## PRAISE FOR SAM CHEEVER

*Sam Cheever creates some of the best characters you could ever find in the pages of a book.*

— SENSUALREADS.COM

*Ms. Cheever writes with class, humor and lots of fun while weaving an excellent story.*

— THE ROMANCE STUDIO

**Loyalties questioned...worlds shaken...nothing is what it seems. LA will have to look beyond her own perceptions to see what's before her very eyes. Or risk losing everything.**

When the barrier between worlds is threatened, LA and her friends are sent into the terrifying realm of *Axismundi* on a super-secret mission to discover who's behind the breaches. LA believes she's going to battle against one of her own...an aunt who's rumored to want multi-dimensional domination.

What she finds once she gets there is nothing like what she expects.

Intrigues swirl. Loyalties change in the blink of an eye. And loss beyond anything she can imagine waits just over the next horizon. Someone is pulling the strings of it all and LA is fighting against the clock to discover who it is.

Can LA get to the bottom of the mystery and save the worlds? Or will she lose what she loves...one friend or family member at a time...and face the crushing end of all she holds dear?

# A FAMILIAR PROBLEM

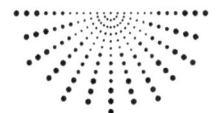

## SAM CHEEVER

ELECTRIC PROSE PUBLICATIONS

# CHAPTER ONE

*A* white-hot blast of pure energy sizzled through the air, so close the tips of my ears burned from the heat. The smell of burning hair and flop sweat filled the air.

Unfortunately, both smells emanated from me.

I tried to see through the haze of smoke to where Deg was huddled. He crouched behind an enormous tree that was newly scored by energy bolts, yellow smoke rising off its wounds and leaving behind a sulfurous stench that burned the eyes and throat.

He straightened, his arm coming up and fingers splayed to emit a golden flash of quelling magic. It would hopefully lock the red-eyed monster across from us into place but leave it alive.

Leaving it alive was imperative. We had to find out what it was and where it had come from.

"Deg!"

He turned to me, frowning. That was when I realized my mistake. We'd been practicing communicating through mental channels but I kept reverting to good old shrieking through the din. It was my comfort zone.

*Sorry*, I told him through our mental pathway. *I'm going to try to get around behind it.*

He nodded, stepping sideways to send dual sprays of spitting silver energy into the air to obscure my movement.

I crouched down and ran, not daring to look toward the line of trees hiding the enormous creature with skin like a rhino and teeth and claws that could sever a limb with a single swipe.

The thing wasn't fooled by Deg's cover for long. As I threw myself behind a large rock, an oily stream of dirty-gray energy sent pieces of the rock into the air and scraped across my calf, dragging a scream from my throat as it burrowed under the skin. The energy hissed happily while it chewed on my flesh.

"*Abortee.*" I murmured as I slapped quelling magic over the wound, extinguishing the evil energy before it could really take hold.

I crawled to my knees and risked a quick glance over the rock.

The thing wasn't where it had been when I'd moved. Panic flared. *Deg?*

*I'm moving to you.*

*Where'd it go?*

*What do you mean? It's behind that tree line.*

*No, it's not….* A wave of rancid air swept over me. I stilled, my fingers flaring with the energy throbbing just beneath my skin.

The atmosphere was sizzling hot, dense with the putrid stench of sulfur. I felt something at my back and, when the low rumble started I didn't need to turn around to know what was there.

"Deg, run!" I whipped around and threw everything I had into the small mountain with the pulsing red eyes. My energy hit the thing and spun, creating a whirlwind of power that seemed unable to breach the monster's protective bubble.

A second strand of magic hit the whirlwind, twining with mine to double the strength.

The creature before me opened its massive jaws. Nasty curved teeth as long as my fingers gleamed in the backlight of our power. The thing looked like it was laughing at us.

That just made me mad.

I screamed as I gave the whirling energy more juice. Slowly the magic made inroads, burning off his dirty-gray magic and sending black sparks that stunk of death into the air.

My knees started to buckle. Flame burst near my cheek and I realized my hair was on fire.

I tried not to panic as agony sizzled over my head and skated down to my shoulders.

The stench of burning hair made my stomach twist with disgust.

My knees hit the ground and the flames slipped down my arms, riding the air above me by such an infinitesimal distance I could feel the heat but wasn't getting burned. I wondered if Deg was experiencing the same phenomena but didn't dare risk a look.

I was quickly losing power. I knew within seconds I'd be flat on my face, helpless against the thing standing before me.

The magical battle had filled the air near the monster with a snowy haze, obscuring everything around it. The haze shimmered as if it were alive. Pulsing toward the monster and then away. I blinked as a small, pale face with pretty blue eyes appeared in its midst and thought I was losing my mind. It looked like a little girl. She wore a shimmering white gown and something that looked like wings danced above her narrow shoulders. Her placid expression seeped into me, calming the frantic beating of my heart.

My magic stuttered and I had to force myself to concentrate or risk losing it.

Smiling calmly, the figure in the mist lifted her small hands, her gaze locked on mine. The haze bulged outward around the monster and, after a heartbeat of hesitation, wrapped around him and sucked him away, leaving behind only an outraged bellow.

I dropped to the ground as if I'd been shot. A soft grunt nearby told me Deg had hit the ground too. I lay there, panting and so weak I could barely move.

"Are you all right?" Deg's voice was scratchy with weariness.

I took a moment to decide. "No. I don't think I am. What in the name of all my ancestors was that thing?"

Deg crawled over and dropped to his butt, leaning his back against the rock I'd been hiding behind. "I have no idea. But the more important question is, what was that thing that took it away?"

Forcing myself off the ground, I leaned against the rock next to him. I lay my head back, my chest heaving. I didn't even want to tell him what I thought I'd seen. I was either crazy or I had an issue I had to deal with that wasn't going to take me to my happy place. "What did it look like to you?"

"Like a cloudy window with nothing behind it."

"Nothing?" I gave him a tired smile. "How do you see nothing?"

"Easy, just look for the absence of something."

We sat in silence for a moment, trying to garner enough energy to climb to our feet. Finally, Deg touched my arm. "We need to go talk to the council. They're going to have to come up with a plan."

I nodded and let him draw me to my feet. But as we stumbled wearily to my elderly MG, I couldn't help wondering if the council members were going to do any better than Deg and I had. It seemed the harder we tried, the more sub-world cockroaches spilled through the cracks.

I was starting to lose hope we'd ever get it under control. And I didn't like the outlook for the world if we didn't.

I just wasn't used to seeing my mother sitting in the center chair at the council table. It gave me a start every time I walked into the enormous room. The twelve people sitting behind the long, black table wore crimson robes with stiff, white collars and identical pinched looks on their faces.

Except, of course, for my mother. She looked stunning as usual. Mother fixed a concerned look on me as I approached the table. The room was empty except for the council members, the decision had been made to keep the current problem as quiet as possible until we could figure out what was going on.

It was a *need to know* situation.

Deg and I stopped before the table and bowed our heads.

After the appropriate moment, mother nodded. "Speak please."

The 'please' was a modern addition. In a time when most of us bristled at the idea of royal-like behavior, even the leaders of our many magical groups were sensitive to being over dictatorial.

"We ran the thing to ground in *Illusory Park*," I told the table. I did my best to ignore the shocked expressions around the table. I really wished they were shocked because of the monster making its way into the park that anchors and protects the magic world around *Illusion City*, but I knew better.

They were appalled that I'd spoken before "my" Witch spoke.

I tipped my chin up and met them in the eye, one by one. Deg and I were ushering in a new era of Witch-Familiar relations. We were a partnership.

"It nearly overcame us," Deg added, frowning.

"Even our combined powers did nothing to stop it," I said.

"Perhaps that's because you aren't properly joined," offered the snotty Witch at my mother's side.

*Serena.* The High Priestess of the coven for the human realm didn't like me or my family. She thought Familiars should know their place, which was of course *beneath* their Witch. Not literally, of course, but if that happened Serena was okay with it. Especially if it suppressed our independence.

Serena had been after Deg to force the joining ritual every Witch and Familiar throughout time had submitted to. Except for us.

The ceremony was heavy on *obey* and *follow* rhetoric. I was having none of that. Despite the fact that most modern Witch-Familiar couples basically worked side by side as equals, ignoring the dictates of the ritual.

I felt like even saying the words took too much away from my identity and I just couldn't suck it down.

Deg understood. He didn't care about the ritual either. But his High Priestess was doing her best to make him miserable in an attempt to cow him.

She fixed me with a sour look, her narrow, cadaverous face made even more haggard by the disgusted puckering of her thin lips. "You haven't realized your full potential yet. You won't until you succumb to the blood-letting ritual."

Yeah, that was the other reason I didn't want to do it. I don't go for unnecessary blood-letting. So pre-historic.

I gave her a too-sweet smile. "Deg and I share a very strong bond, Serena. There was no magical malfunction. That…thing was just too strong."

Deg nodded thoughtfully. "It was like its energy came from somewhere else. Not of this world."

Silence fell around the table. Eyes widened and several of the council members shared looks. My mother's gaze stayed fixed on mine. Too fixed.

She wasn't even blinking.

They knew something Deg and I didn't. That irritated the pants off me. Good thing I was wearing a skirt. "Is there something we should know?" My voice was determinedly sweet, like the smile I spread around the table, but I was met with pinched lips and stern gazes.

*I really hate these people*, I told Deg.

He threw me a look. "Madam Queen," he addressed my mother. "We'd like your permission to perform some tracking magics in the park."

That surprised my mother's gaze, finally, from mine. "Tracking magics? Why?"

The answer to that seemed obvious to me but Deg was more political than I was.

"The creature was enveloped by some sort of haze. It felt almost like a barrier of some kind."

Mother blinked. "Explain."

"It was like there was a barrier within the barrier," I said brusquely. I wanted to see their reactions.

*Illusory Park* had two areas. The area non-magics saw, which looked just like a regular park, made up of grass, trees and even a pretty lake in the center. Then there was the side the human population would never see. The side that served as both protection and escape for magical beings in the area.

The barrier that kept the two areas separate was fed by all of us, the combined magics interwoven to be a million times stronger than any single magic user's power could be.

"You're saying this creature breached our barrier?" Mother asked on a frown.

"No." I shook my head. "We're saying it breached a secondary barrier within the forest."

Someone gasped and general murmuring ensued. Deg and I waited it out, reading their expressions and posture. What I saw was fear and shock, but not surprise.

The ruling council had known that internal barrier was there.

Interesting.

*Are you seeing what I'm seeing*, Deg asked.

*Yeah*, I answered. *They knew*. Aloud I said, "So, why don't you tell us what this internal barrier is, and why this creature lives behind it, so Deg and I can do the job you asked us to do?"

The room went unnaturally still.

Every gaze burned over me, filled with hostility and just a tiny bit of fear.

The hostility I was used to. The fear unsettled me. What did this magical barrier represent?

My mother skimmed a look down the table, probably trying to assess the general mood. I could have saved her the trouble. The general mood was stinky, bordering on cranky and downright irritable.

She glanced at me and quickly away, choosing to focus her response on Deg instead. I bristled, thinking it was a hierarchy thing...then I realized it was even more despicable than that.

It was a mother-daughter thing.

"It's not a barrier," she told Deg.

I opened my mouth and she stabbed a finger into the air to stop me.

"It's a dimensional wall."

My mouth closed with an audible snap. I heard Deg swallow. He cleared his throat and I realized he didn't know how to respond.

*Holy crap!* Probably wasn't an appropriate response to a room filled with cantankerous and uber-powerful magical beings.

"What's a dimensional barrier doing in *Illusory Park?*"

All eyes sifted to me and I fought the urge to shift nervously. "It's a fair question. I've never heard of one opening up there before. Don't they usually only open when there's a breach in the magic – non-magic balance?"

The response came to me in a much deeper voice than I'd expected. My gaze slid down the table, where a hole in the line of crabby faces made me almost smile. Slowly, Alabast, the Demon King, eased his weight forward, fixing a dark and amused gaze on me. He actually smiled then, and I saw a brief flash of his nephew Brock in his handsome features. "LA."

I inclined my head, "King Alabast."

"As usual you've managed to cut right to the heart of the matter." His black gaze scanned to my mother and hung there. "Queen Katherine believes that if we ignore the problem it will go away."

My mother's shoulders stiffened and she clenched her hand around the pen lying on the table in front of her. "That's not true, Al and you know it. I've put out feelers…"

The demon laughed. "Feelers? How many of them came back alive?"

Mother frowned. "I'm handling it."

But the demon king was every bit as determined as his nephew, and probably just as annoying too. He rested muscular arms on the table and bent his head to glance down the long line of silent council members. "This isn't just a Familiar problem, Katherine. If the afterlife dimension has descended on *Illusion City*, it's a problem for all of us."

I felt my eyes go wide. "After…"

My mother cut me off. "I said...!" she screamed, her pretty face darkening with rage. "I'm handling it."

"Let's be civil, Katherine," said an elderly woman whose head barely cleared the table, even though I knew from prior experience that she was sitting on a child's booster seat. The Queen of the Sprites was tiny even for a Sprite, but nothing about her demeanor revealed it.

Only the dangling feet beneath the table brought it brutally home.

"We know you're dealing with the problem. But we all have a right to participate in the delegation. She'll expect to see a representative from each of the magical houses."

My mother frowned. She was clearly not happy, but I could tell she knew the others were right. "Let's discuss it later." She turned to Deg and me. "Thank you for your report. I'll be in touch."

I started to argue but Deg grabbed my arm, giving it a gentle tug. *They're not going to tell us anything. We'll need to figure out what's going on for ourselves.*

He was right. Besides, I knew from experience that we couldn't trust what the council members told us anyway. More than half the time they told us what they thought we expected to hear, instead of the truth.

I followed Deg out of the room, suddenly eager to get out of that place and back to my own little sanctuary.

A cat rescue might not be exciting or adventurous, but I loved my work and all the critters I was able to help.

It was a good life.

I had a momentary spurt of happiness that carried me outside to the street.

Then I remembered that *Axismundi*, the afterlife dimension, was hovering around *Illusory Park*.

And I couldn't help wondering if the afterlife had come to pick up anybody I knew and loved.

# CHAPTER TWO

*M*andy shook her head, her caramel-colored gaze narrowed in thought. "I've never heard of that. Are you sure they said it was a dimension?"

I nodded but she wasn't looking at me. She had her attention fixed firmly on her ex, and Deg was returning the favor. I suddenly felt like the third wheel I no doubt was. "Not just another dimension he responded. But an afterlife dimension. What exactly does that mean? Have you heard anything that would suggest an emergence of *Axismundi* in the middle of a human dimension?"

"Technically, it *wasn't* a human dimension though, was it?" Mandy said as if thinking it through. "It was inside the *Illusory Park* barrier."

I shook my head. "I'm sorry, I'm having trouble picturing Hades as something that just floats around like a fiery dirigible, puking underworld creatures out on unsuspecting worlds without reason or notice."

Mandy finally favored me with a snotty glance. "It's not like that. *Axismundi* is everywhere. It sits inside and around all dimensions. Which is why the critter you fought was something we've never seen before. It probably came from a totally other dimension."

"Wait," Deg frowned "I'm starting to remember something we learned in school…"

"Hogwarts?" I asked, grinning.

The two Witches didn't even acknowledge me or my little joke.

"Isn't *Axismundi* sort of a massive *Illusory Park?*"

"Pretty? With a pond?" I asked.

"No." Mandy responded, giving me a withering look. "It's a portal, just as the park is here. We can reach any part of *Illusion City* through the barrier in the park, right?"

Deg nodded. "Okay, I get it."

"Well I don't," I objected. "What is *Axismundi* a portal to?"

Mandy cocked a hip, her dark brows lowering. "To your life, clearly." She glared around at my messy kitchen, where I'd been cooking up some spells before they so rudely interrupted me. Admittedly, it did look like a level five tornado had come through. But I'd been very productive and I was sure we were going to need the spells I'd made very soon.

Deg scowled Mandy's way. "*Axismundi* leads to all the other dimensions."

My eyes went wide. "So, if we wanted to get to another dimension…"

He nodded. "Theoretically, we could cut through the afterworld to do it."

"Cool," I said in a voice filled with awe.

"You wouldn't think so if you'd ever been inside the place," Mandy said. She rubbed a perfectly manicured finger over the counter in front of her and grimaced, examining the fingertip as if she'd accidentally touched cat poop.

I frowned. Had I used cat poop in that last concoction?

"All that is moot," Deg said on a sigh. "We wouldn't know what, or who, we were looking for anyway. Unless the council comes clean about what's going on, we're stuck."

"They're not going to tell us anything," I told him. "I know my mother. When she gets that stubborn look on her face you couldn't pull a secret out of her with a dredging spell."

My doorbell rang and the door immediately slammed back against the wall. In a flash, Mandy, Deg and I all had magic spitting from our fingertips.

"Hello?"

Hearing the well-known voice, I relaxed slightly. My visitor wasn't a threat. I didn't think. But we stayed in defense mode just in case.

Though, in our defense, we did let the magic slide away as my mother glided into the room.

She stopped just inside the door and scoured the room with a horrified gaze. "LeeAnn? What's going on here?"

"I'm working. The bigger question is, why are you here?"

She closed her mouth and frowned. "Can't I come visit my daughter?"

"Yes. But usually I know you're coming."

Mother shrugged. "Fair point." She smiled at Deg and Mandy. "Hello."

Mandy had paled when my mother walked into the room. For the first time since I'd met her, the cocky Witch seemed at a loss for words.

Deg smiled. "Hey, Queen Katherine."

"Just Katherine will do. My mother's the queen. I'm just filling in for her until she gets back on her feet."

A dark wave of worry swept through me. My Grand-mama, Celeste, was the most powerful Familiar in the magic world. Some believed she was as powerful as Serena, which might explain the sour Witch's antipathy toward the Mapes family. Celeste had taken quite a hit, both magically and physically as it turned out, when a rogue Familiar had nearly managed to gain control of the powerful common web that tied us all together.

It had taken every bit of magic Celeste, my mother, Deg, Mandy, I and even Brock had been able to cobble together to stop the rogue.

Six months later, Celeste still hadn't recovered.

I suddenly realized we were all just standing there staring at each other and gave myself a mental nudge. "Would you like some tea or…something? I have cookies."

A smile transformed my mother's beautiful face, like the sun coming out from behind a thick bank of clouds. "I'd like that, Peaches. Thank you."

As I turned, I caught Mandy's gaze and she mouthed, *Peaches?* Humor lighting her gaze.

"Shut up," I told her softly.

Deg brought the pitcher of sweet iced tea from the fridge and poured four glasses as I filled a plate with homemade chocolate chip cookies. My mother walked around the room, checking out my messy kitchen. I expected a lecture on tidiness from the woman who never had a hair out of place. But instead she stopped in front of the double row of bottles containing my cooling spells. "You've been busy."

I placed the cookies in the center of my little round kitchen table and Deg placed a small tray with the pitcher and glasses next to it. "After dealing with that thing in the park I thought I'd better get more prepared."

Mother turned, smiling. "That's my girl." She pointed to a tiny jar filled with black air. "Is this…?"

"Invisibilia," I nodded. "Flavored with an aura cleanse."

Her eyes went wide. "Smart. How long will it last?"

"Twenty minutes," Mandy said, grabbing a cookie and dropping into a chair. "She used my recipe."

Mother redirected her gaze to the Witch. "I'd like a copy if I might?"

"Of course." Mandy's smile was genuine, one of the few I'd ever seen from her. "I also make a mean growth spell. It transforms to twice normal size within thirty seconds and lasts almost an hour."

"Ingenious." Mother nodded thoughtfully. "If you'd like, come down to *Familiar, Inc.* next week and let's talk. I'd like the Witches in my lab to look at them. Maybe we can manufacture some of your spells in large quantities for sale to the larger magic population. I'd reimburse you of course."

Mandy hid her smile behind the cookie. "We can talk."

I handed mother a small plate with a cookie and a glass of tea. She took it gratefully, drinking a third of the tea down immediately. She followed that with a bite of cookie. "This is perfect, LA. I didn't have time for breakfast or lunch today. The council has been in non-stop meeting mode trying to figure out what to do about the mess in the park."

Deg and I shared a look. Apparently, even though they weren't surprised about the existence of the *Axismundi* dimension in *Illusory Park*, the council members were concerned about its recent activities. "Mom, I know you don't want to tell us what's going on..."

She shook her head before I could even complete the sentence and I bit back frustration with a tinge of anger. The lack of trust from the magic world was one of the big reasons I'd kept to myself until recently. When Deg had come into my life.

If I thought finally bonding with a Witch was going to make them accept me, I'd clearly been wrong.

"On the contrary, I want the four of you to go on a secret mission for me."

I blinked several times, shocked. "Secret mission?"

"Yes." She put the half-eaten cookie on the table, wiping

her fingers on a clean paper napkin. "Into *Axismundi*. There's someone there I need you to speak to. And...this is important..." she told us, capturing the gaze of each of us in turn. "No one else can know about this."

*Don't hit me with a feather*, Deg mumbled in my mind. *I'll probably fall over.*

*Right?* I responded breathlessly. I narrowed my gaze on mother. "Let me get this straight. You're sending us into the *Axismundi* dimension without the other council members' knowledge?"

"Yes. No one except for King Al. He agrees with me that we need to be proactive in this."

"Not that I want to talk you out of it but...why?"

"Because you four are the only ones I can really trust."

Okay, I was clearly an ass. But I was a touched ass. Wait... that didn't sound right. I was touched by my mother's trust. *And* I was an ass for thinking the worst of her a moment earlier.

"Wait," Mandy said. "Four of us? Who's the fourth?"

"I'm guessing that would be me."

We all turned to the tall, dark figure in the doorway. "Demon. How'd you get into my house?"

"Um...I walked through the unlocked and slightly ajar door."

I glared over at my mother.

"Sorry. I didn't know you wanted it locked." She shrugged, grabbing her cookie and taking another dainty bite. She chewed and swallowed as Brock joined us at the table, grabbing three cookies without being invited.

That seemed to be a theme with him.

"So, what's going on?" He asked the room at large.

We all looked at mother and she swallowed, swiping a napkin across her lips. She held my gaze and hesitated, clearly reluctant to tell me who we were going into *Axis-mundi* to see.

"Mother?"

"Trudy Hawthorne Mapes."

I blinked. The name sounded vaguely recognizable but I couldn't place it for a moment. Then my eyes went wide. "Aunt Trudy?"

Mother nodded, her expression carefully neutral. "Good. You remember her. I wasn't sure you would."

I really remembered mostly impressions. A wide smile, pretty gray-blue eyes that always glinted with something that looked like madness. Pinching... I frowned. "Why do I remember pinching?"

Mother grimaced. "Trudy was fond of pinching."

"As punishment?" the demon asked, grinning.

"No." Mother shook her head. "She just liked to pinch."

"Alrighty then," Mandy said, sneering. "I can't wait to meet her."

Always the practical one, Deg got right to the point. "Why are we meeting Trudy?"

Mother eased herself wearily into a chair. She reached out and ran a blood-red tipped nail over the condensation in her glass of sweet tea. It was another long moment before she spoke. "This is a very sensitive subject for the council. They've tried to ignore it for years but of course it isn't going away." A fly buzzed past and, frowning, mother drew a bug repelling hex on the table with the liquid from the tea. The fly shot sideways and out the door, probably through my front door, which I had no doubt the demon had left open.

Thus, the fly in the first place.

"Mother?" I tried again.

She sighed. "Trudy has some strange ideas about the hier-archy between the different houses in the magical world. She was devoted to recreating the interrelationships throughout her entire life and...well...her time in the afterlife doesn't seem to have changed that."

"What do you mean recreating interrelationships?" I asked.

"Trudy believes in a flat magical society. She doesn't recognize dark or light, good or bad. But it goes even deeper than that. Trudy believes the lowliest gargoyle should have the same influence into the decisions and actions of the magical world as do the highest magic houses. She recognizes no pecking order between Witches and Familiars." She glanced at Brock. "She wants to obliterate the demonic hierarchy too."

He frowned. "But that would create..."

"Chaos," mother nodded. "And worse. Our ability to protect humankind will be destroyed."

I was starting to understand why Mother was desperate enough to send us into *Axismundi*. "But she has no real control, right? The council regulates those types of decisions."

"Based on a millennia of practice and process," Deg added.

"Traditionally, that is correct. But Trudy's been in *Axismundi* for a decade now. She's been working behind the scenes to create the world she wants. And I fear she's going to move soon to force it on the rest of us."

"Force?" Mandy asked, frowning. "How?"

"You've already begun to see it happen," Mother told us.

"The strange monsters," Deg said.

"From other dimensions. Yes," Mother agreed. "If she gets what she wants, there will no longer be separate dimensions. Trudy will intermingle them in one, uncontrolled blast. We'll be overrun with creatures we can't hope to understand or control."

"The humans will get caught in the crossfire," I breathed,

horrified. I met my mother's fear-filled gaze. "We need to stop her."

"Exactly."

"But why not tell the council what we're doing?" Deg asked. "Surely they don't support her actions."

"Most don't. But I'm sure you can understand that some of the houses which have been held to the lower rungs in the hierarchy might embrace this plan."

Unfortunately, I *could* see that. Very clearly.

"What about the rest of *Axismundi*?" Mandy asked. "Are they all supportive of Trudy's plan?"

"No. Fortunately we do have allies there. Some of them have even begun slipping through the barrier between *Axismundi* and the human dimension, working quietly behind the scenes."

"Can we work directly with them to keep Trudy's plan from bleeding into this dimension?" Brock asked.

"That would be a fond dream," mother said. "Unfortunately, they risk everything to help. Trudy's amassed a huge amount of power in *Axismundi*. If she gets even a whiff of a rebellion..."

"She'll go postal on their derrieres," Mandy said on a frown.

"I'm certain they'll reveal themselves in time. But, for now, we're on our own."

"What exactly do you want us to do when we meet with Aunt Trudy," I asked my mom.

"Just talk to her. Find out what she's planning if you can. But whatever you do, don't take sides. Don't do anything to make her think you're on the side of the rebellion. Do what you have to do to make her believe you're totally neutral. You're not there to judge. Only to get information for me." Mother reached out and clasped my hand. Her fingers were soft and cold as ice. "It will mean the difference between life and death, LA. I'm not exaggerating at all when I say that."

I nodded. "Got it. I'm Switzerland."

Mother didn't share my smile. She stood up. "Good. You'll leave in the morning, before first light. I'll meet you in the park and help you create a break between the barriers. From there it will be up to you."

## CHAPTER THREE

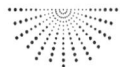

"*M*aybe we should just let gargoyles rule," Brock grumbled the next morning, his jaw cracking on a massive yawn.

Mandy shoved an enormous coffee into his hand. "That's the lack of caffeine talking. Drink."

Brock did drink, but then he shook his head. "No. It's the lack of sleep talking. Why couldn't this wait until a decent hour. Even the chickens aren't up yet."

"Because we're trying to fly under the radar," I told the grumbly demon. I looked around, worry gnawing at me as the hour grew later and my mother still hadn't arrived.

"She's fine, LA," Deg told me. "I'm sure she just got waylaid by one of the council members. She doesn't want to be seen coming here to meet us."

But I didn't believe him. Something cold and slimy had moved into my bones, dread and…fear. "Something's happened. I can feel it."

Mandy frowned. "Should we go to the tower?"

"No." I didn't know what was going on, but my instincts were screaming at me that the only chance we had of helping my mother and…quite possibly…the rest of the world, was to move forward. "We stick to the plan."

"Okay," Brock grumbled. "Do you know how to create a breach in the barriers, because I don't."

We fell silent, all of us looking everywhere but at each other. Nobody knew how to do what we needed to do. And that was a problem.

"Maybe we should try to reach her through the web," Deg finally suggested. "Or your grandmother."

I shook my head. "No. It's too dangerous."

"Then…?" Mandy said, lifting slender, dark brows in hostile question.

*Meow…*

A small form wound itself around my feet and ankles. I glanced down, expecting to see Mabel, one of three tiny kittens I'd recently rescued from an alley in *Illusion City*. To my surprise it was her brother. The tiger striped orange cat with startling yellow eyes. "Ralph?"

He looked up at me as I said his name and gave me a creaky meow, as if his voice was still rusty with sleep. He dropped to his butt and cocked his head, his eyes squinting as he purred. The throaty rumble of his contented purring filled the otherwise quiet dawn. The grass rustled beside a thick birch tree and another small form trotted out of the shadows.

Energy crackled on Mandy and Deg's fingertips but I threw out a hand to stop them. "It's only Mack, Ralph's brother." The smaller charcoal gray male ran up and threw himself at my legs, rubbing his face over my calf. His purring joined his brother's until the noise was uncomfortably loud. "Keep it down, you two," I whispered. "This is a secret mission."

"What is it with those kittens?" Mandy asked "They always seem to turn up when we have a crisis."

I crouched down and scooped up Mack, letting him rub his head over my chin as I snuggled him close. The brief moment made me feel more calm.

Down at my ankles, Ralph was doing tight figure eights, his short, thick tail smacking softly against my skin.

The air near my shoulder snapped with electricity and Mack meowed again, the husky sound turning into a growl with a quick hiss at the end.

A slender ray of sizzling gold energy made a vertical slash against the pre-dawn darkness.

"The barrier!" Mandy said. Immediately her hands came up and she started drawing symbols on the air. The spell glowed bright for a moment in the darkness, each symbol flaring to life and then fading away as she worked some kind of spell.

Deg joined in, his magic flaring against hers in long silver streaks that wound in circular patterns around each symbol and then sent sparks into the air as they disappeared.

I stepped back as the glowing golden portal in the air widened and flashed, showing a deep, dense darkness beyond its edges. It pulsed and throbbed, going nearly closed one moment and then flaring wider the next.

Mandy and Deg scribed frantically on the air, their faces dark with intensity.

The sun rose slowly toward the tops of the distant trees, and beyond the spit and sizzle of building magic, the sound of morning birds followed its golden rise. A gentle pinkness spread across the horizon and I knew we were running out of time.

Dawn was coming.

Sweat glistened on Deg's forehead. Lines of weariness showed in thin furrows between Mandy's brows. I started to panic.

"What can I do to help?" I asked Deg.

He shook his head, too busy to speak. So, I fell back on our training together and reached out, letting my energy roll in silvery strands from my fingertips. My magic headed unerringly toward his and burst, emitting light and energy in a backwash to send Deg and Mandy stumbling back.

"Too much?" I asked with a grimace.

The two Witches breathed heavily, their hands drooping as their energy died a quick death.

"It's no use," Mandy said. "I can't crank it open. We must be missing something."

I eyed the pink and purple horizon, feeling my stress returning. Ralph gave an angry yowl and scratched my hand, leaping from my grip and hitting the grass mere inches from the quickly closing barrier.

"Ouch!" I yelled, sucking the torn flesh into my mouth. "That hurt," I complained.

Ralph didn't seem to care. He was sniffing the breach, all the hair on his back lifting as his brother casually sauntered over and joined him.

"Get them away from that!" Deg yelled.

I realized as he yelled that the two kittens were in terrible danger. I jumped toward them, my hands reaching for them as I screamed. "No!"

But it was too late. The kittens shoved their noses into the breach and were sucked inside with a surprised yowl.

I stood there for a moment, staring helplessly at the atmospheric tear, and then made a frustrated sound, stepping toward the breach.

"Don't do it, LA. You won't survive…"

I didn't wait to hear the end of Deg's warning. I slipped a hand into the tear and screamed as something grabbed me in a brutal grip and yanked me through.

# CHAPTER FOUR

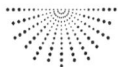

*I* flew through the air and hit the ground hard, my bones bashing against a ragged surface of dirt and rock. Dust flew up all around me as I rolled to a stop several feet from the breach.

I coughed, my lungs contracting on the silty dust. My eyes stung and watered so badly I couldn't see.

Something foul and poisonous filled the black-as-night atmosphere.

"Sulfur," said a voice I didn't recognize.

I jerked in surprise, fighting to clear my vision.

The unmistakable sound of sizzling energy brought me to my feet, magic dancing along my fingertips as I used my sleeve to scrub at my watery gaze in an effort to clear it.

Something hit the ground near my feet and barreled into me, taking me down again. The energy of the breach snapped again and another heavy form hit the dirt nearby. I folded protectively into myself, trying not to get hit with another flying body, but nothing came barreling my way.

Crumpled up next to me, Deg groaned. "Well that sucked."

"It wasn't exactly a smooth entrance," Brock agreed a few feet away.

I scrubbed my sleeve across my eyes again and finally managed to crank them open. It was so dark that, for a beat I thought my lids were still closed.

As my vision adjusted, I turned to Deg and found him trying to dig something shaped like small rocks out of his elbows. I grimaced. "That must hurt."

"Yeah."

The breach sizzled again and we all flinched. It widened just enough to allow Mandy to walk gracefully through. She looked down her long nose at us, clearly disgusted by our messy, ungraceful sprawls. "I hope you three brought a change of clothes."

I looked down at my clothes, realizing I could kind of see the brown smears on my jeans through the dim light.

"Welcome to *Axismundi*."

Yelping in an unmanly way, I threw out my hands, energy flying to dance at my fingertips. I'd momentarily forgotten about the voice.

Deg and Brock surged to their feet, their own magic sizzling.

Mandy rolled her eyes. "If he wanted to kill us you three would already be dead."

The slender, dark haired youth standing a few yards away nodded. "She's right. I'm here to help."

He had bright orange hair with strange black highlights and a small frame. I judged him to be around eleven, but his green eyes were filled with an intelligence far greater than his years.

We all stared at him another beat and then let our magic leak away. Deg offered me a hand up and I took it. Brushing dirt from my clothes as best I could, I addressed the young man. "Did you see a couple of kittens come through right before me?"

"They followed my brother that way."

I glanced in the direction he indicated, noticing for the first time the throbbing glow lighting up the distant sky. "Where was your brother going?" All I could think of was getting those kittens back. They'd be helpless against the types of creatures they might encounter in that place.

Who was I kidding? My friends and I were probably helpless against most of them.

"He's heading to the event."

"What event?" Brock asked, frowning.

"The weekly coronation event."

Deg and I shared a look. "Weekly?" I asked.

He shrugged. "That's kind of an inside joke, actually. We've been trying to coronate her for a couple of decades but somebody always invades during the ceremony." He shook his head. "I've lost more friends in those invasions."

"Who are we talking about coronating?" Mandy asked.

He scoured us with a look filled with disbelief. "Did the council tell you nothing?"

"Not nothing exactly…" I began. But then I couldn't really isolate a single thing my mother had told me about what we were walking into except that Trudy, my dead aunt, was probably at the center of the problem.

"Pretty much nothing, yeah," we all agreed at once.

The young man expelled air. "Well, that certainly makes my job harder."

"Um…sorry?" I asked.

Mandy shook her dark head, frowning. "The council members aren't the only ones telling us nothing."

Brock nodded. "Yeah. Who are you and what exactly *is* your job?"

"I'm Deer and I'm supposed to take you to the resistance."

"Deer?" Deg asked with lifted brows.

"It's my code name." When they didn't immediately respond with understanding noises, he clarified. "Because I can run fast."

"Ah," I said. "So, Deer, here's the thing. We don't want to go to the resistance. I need to speak to Aunt Trudy right away. There can be no suspicion at all that I'm with any resistance. I can't risk it."

Deer looked confused. "Aunt...?" his expression darkened with anger. "You're siding with her?"

Energy flared from young Deer, creating a golden aura that surrounded his entire form.

Deg held up his hands. "Whoa, there, Deer. Nobody said that. But we were given very specific orders." His expression turned harsh. "And let's be clear. We don't know you from Adam. You could be a spy sent to test us."

"Adam? Who is this Adam?"

Brock rolled his eyes. "Just point us in Trudy's direction and we'll get out of your very orange hair. Then you can catch up with your brother, Pig or Zebra, or whatever his name is."

Our would-be guide's aura flared up again. His hands clenched and his expression turned dark and cold, making him look like an angry statue.

I glared at Brock. "Not helping, demon."

The demon just shook his head.

"We're outsiders. Consider us neutral observers for now. We only want to talk to her. We're trying to figure out her plans for our dimension. Can you help us get an audience?"

Deer stared at me for a long moment and then shook his head. "I won't be any part of helping you support the Nemesis Trudy." He started to turn away and stopped. "But I will give you one piece of advice. Don't tell anyone she's your aunt. That information will get you killed faster than a stroll through *Demon Hill*. And you won't have just one enemy here in *Axismundi*, you'll have nearly endless enemies. That idiot woman isn't creating the flat hierarchy she thinks she is, she's creating a world filled with chaos. And if she gets her way that chaos will spread across the twelve dimensions. Then we'll all be victims of her stupid plans."

He disappeared in a flash of light, leaving us standing in stunned silence. Hearing about the potential pandemonium of Trudy's plan from my mother while safely ensconced in my normal and predictable world was one thing. But hearing about it when standing in a strange and hostile dimension where I'd just been told everyone wanted to kill me was quite another.

"So, what now?" Brock asked in a rumbly voice.

I glanced at him and saw the slight red glow behind his eyes and the muted smolder of his aura that told me he was in defensive mode.

Deg was silent, his lack of comment concerning. Especially when I looked at him and found him frowning toward the razor thin breach. I could feel his yearning to return through that intangible strand of light. But I knew he wouldn't act on it.

He was the most determined and responsible Witch I knew.

"LA?"

I blinked, realizing my friends were waiting for me to respond to Brock's question. "Oh. Um." I pointed toward the distant glow in the sky. "We head that way. I'm guessing that light has something to do with the coronation. That's where we'll find Aunt Trudy."

Only problem was, I just wasn't convinced that *finding* her was a very smart thing to do.

THE GROUND beneath our feet crunched loudly as we walked. Every crunch echoed into the darkness, falling away with a heavy thud as it hit the alien and curiously thick atmosphere. The ground was black, as if every inch of the place had been charred into permanent death. But it sifted beneath my feet like sand, a nearly non-existent light glinting off its surface at random moments.

There was no moon in the sky above us. No light at all except for the pulsing illumination on the distant horizon. But somehow my eyes had adjusted enough to see the occasional shape rising up around us as we moved slowly through the limitless dark.

There were no recognizable trees or other vegetation.

Here and there something that might have once been green and alive lifted barren branches toward the black umbrella above, a testament to what might have been vibrant in an earlier time.

My head was on a constant swivel as I walked. Needles of horrified anticipation stabbed a constant warning between my shoulder blades.

I imagined that I could feel a hundred gazes on me, obscured in the all-but-total darkness, and wondered when the first attack would come.

From my friends' silence...and their constantly roving gazes...I could tell they felt the same danger in the air.

Something drifted by, leaving an icy prickle on my face. It was like a sigh. A whisper. But it was thick with malice and dragged me to an alarmed stop, energy sparking from my hands.

"What is it?" Deg asked, his gaze sliding uselessly around the night.

"I felt something," I whispered.

Behind us, Mandy jumped, giving a breathy yelp of fear. "What was that?"

Beside her, Brock's aura flared brighter. His eyes glowed eerily though the dark. "I sense demons."

"Just perfect," I muttered under my breath.

The stench of sulfur thickened. The air heated noticeably. We all stood very still, formed in a circle without even thinking, with our backs to the center. Energy pulsed at our fingertips and I didn't have to look at Brock to know he'd taken his demonic form. I'd seen it only once and it was terrifying.

I only hoped it was enough to frighten whatever stalked us.

The whisper of sound surged past again, bringing with it a biting wave of static that made every hair on my body rise to attention.

Deg murmured softly beside me. And behind him, Mandy whispered magical words that sent fiery orange symbols dancing on the air. The symbols she and Deg formed with their quickly moving fingers danced around each other, forming into a ring of energy that encompassed all four of us.

As the warding snapped into place, some of the dread I'd been feeling softened, muffled behind a wall of protective magics.

The silence between us grew, became oppressive. Anxious to complete our mission and get the Hades out of there, I fought the urge to break through the ward and just start running, firing energy at anything that moved.

But the others held me there. I didn't want to do anything to jeopardize their safety. So, I dug for patience and held firm, my gaze locked on the area around our small group.

Nothing stirred.

No movement.

No sound.

There was only the skin-prickling feeling of being stalked.

Then the darkness shifted.

The warding surrounding us stretched with an ear-splitting scream and I stumbled back, bumping up against Mandy as she and Deg chanted louder, their fingers moving so fast they were a blur on the night.

The warding snapped again, sending reverberations through the space inside it and, as if someone had shot a starting gun at a gargoyle race, the blackness exploded into motion.

# CHAPTER FIVE

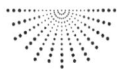

*T*he screams curdled my blood. Reacting in genuine fear and on the heels of pure adrenaline, we all scrambled backward. The warded circle snapped smaller to contain us.

The air thickened with the stench of sulfur and rot and the frantic activity beyond our circle spun it around and over us, filling our nostrils with the reek of death.

But the screaming and the stink were nothing compared to what we were seeing.

Horrid, black-eyed faces with yellowed skin and sunken cheeks, and black stringy lips pulled back to show a terrifying set of deadly fangs. Gray, curved teeth rose up from the narrow jaws and even bigger fangs curved down to meet them.

Saliva dripped from the fangs and sizzled like acid on the black ground.

They had long bodies with humanoid arms and shoulders and a bird's tail. The feathers on their raven-like wings looked like they'd been oiled, a jagged fringe which wildly thrashed the air, sending their stink to invade our little safe space.

*Harpies!*

My heart was pounding so hard I felt lightheaded. For one, horrifying moment I thought I would pass out from fear.

The creatures slammed into the warding, its invisible walls shuddering under the impact as several of them hit us at once. They screeched constantly, the sound slicing against our hearing like razor-sharp blades. I threw my hands over my tortured ears and fought to keep standing as my brain turned to mush and blood leaked from between my fingers.

Between shrieks Deg and Mandy's chanting grew louder, turning hoarse as the flying monsters beat relentlessly against their ward.

I didn't know how they could keep on working their magics. It was all I could do not to break through the doomed warding and run screaming to a certain death.

Apparently, I wasn't alone. Behind me, Brock suddenly flexed, his demonic form breaking free from the protective magic and surging straight up in the air with a rage-filled roar. The circle wobbled dangerously for a beat as Mandy lost her focus and looked up at him. "Brock, no!"

I looked skyward, horror making me forget to breathe.

Deg's voice rose, his fingers flying upon the air, and the protective circle slid closed around the three of us again.

My gaze locked on the enraged demon and, despite myself, I sucked air in an appreciative gasp. Brock was heart-stoppingly gorgeous in a demonic goth kind of way.

He looked down on us, his fierce red gaze blazing like fire in a handsome black face. A thick cap of shiny black hair swept away from a face that I still recognized, splitting to show a pair of very sharp horns before falling in perfect waves down the back of Brock's head and to his broad shoulders.

Brock landed several feet away and the shrieking monsters went very still, watching him with something that looked like awe.

I was with them.

In his demonic form, Brock was ten feet tall and had clawed fingers and thirty-foot-wide, sawtooth-edged wings. He was terrifyingly beautiful.

Power personified.

He was also in horrible, lung-freezing danger as the things that had been attacking the circle gave up on us and started after him.

"I'll draw them off and you run," Brock growled out before leaping off the ground, his massive wings pounding rhythmically as he rose into the black sky.

With a final screech, the creatures that surrounded us followed, streaking straight off the ground so quickly it sucked the breath right out of my lungs.

Panic clawed my chest as the warding dropped away and Deg and Mandy hit their knees, panting and pinch-faced with exhaustion.

"Brock!" I screamed after him. "He'll be killed," I told my friends as I started to run after him.

Deg shoved slowly to his feet, his face gray with fatigue. "Then let's not let it be in vain." He turned to Mandy. "Come on, Witch. Dig deep. We need to get out of here before those things come back."

To her credit, the snarky, know-it-all Witch didn't complain or argue. She allowed Deg to pull her to her feet and, with a final look toward the cacophony of shrieks fading away into the distance, we took off running toward the distant light.

~

IT SEEMED like hours before the horrendous shrieking faded away. It was probably much closer to thirty seconds. But every nerve-crawling screech made me want to scream and hurt something. I had no idea what was happening to my friend.

Brock had basically sacrificed himself so we could live. So we could finish what we'd come to do. If we ever made it home I swore to myself I'd make sure he was honored in some way.

"There!" Deg pointed toward a single glowing object in the near distance. It looked like the remains of a bush, the barren branches wearing black and orange fire instead of leaves. The flames danced silently, giving off no smoke or any discernable scent. It was magic fire, conjured rather than formed of natural things.

I realized after a moment that the bush was one of several reaching off into the distance. It was a pathway of some kind, bending up a hill that seemed to rise toward the horizon.

I jerked to a stop and grabbed Deg's arm. "We need to figure out what this is." I threw out my magics and "felt" the area around us for other life. My energy swept away from me in a purple haze that I knew only I would be able to see. It was tracking magic. Very rare in a Familiar and almost as rare in Witches. I'd used it sparingly all my life, knowing that every use of magic required an equal price that needed to be paid. But I'd be damned if I was walking down the path laid out before us without knowing what was there. The energy jerked to a stop a mere fifty yards away. Much too soon. It had hit a barrier of some kind.

But it seemed to be working inside the limited space. Almost immediately I got the sense of several other creatures. All large, with dark auras.

"Demons," I told my friends. "We need to go around."

Mandy sighed. "But this is the most direct route."

"How many do you sense, LA?" Deg asked.

"Half a dozen. But I seem to only be able to *read* a small area. There could be some kind of dampening magic at work here." I shuddered as a wave of foreboding slipped past, lifting gooseflesh on my arms and bringing the prickling sensation back to rest between my shoulder blades. "We're being watched," I told my friends. "I've felt it since we left the portal."

Mandy nodded. "I have too. But whoever…whatever…it is seems to be tracking us. It might not want to hurt us."

"And the demons waiting along that pathway just want to have tea and cookies with us," I grumbled.

Mandy frowned.

I realized I was being bitchy. She probably didn't know how to react. Being a "Witch with a B" was usually her department. "Sorry. I'm stressed."

Her eyes went wide. "Ya think?"

Suddenly we were laughing together and some of the stress leeched out of the situation. I found that I could breathe and think again. I looked at Deg. "I'm not comfortable taking this pathway without knowing exactly what's waiting for us. They'll be able to see *us* but we can't see *them*."

Deg and Mandy shared a look. They both started talking at once, then fell into a long, whispered conversation using Witchy type words that pretty much flew past my ears on wings of cotton candy.

I didn't understand anything except the words, *The Blend*, which they kept repeating.

Finally, I lost my temper. "Hello?"

They turned to me, grinning. Mandy reached into her pocket and pulled out a small bag filled with prickly green stuff. Holding it up she said. "I brought it just in case."

I shook my head. "You want to get high right now? I'm thinking that might be a bad idea. Call me overly cautious."

"No LA, that's not a drug. It's *The Blend*," Deg told me.

I lifted my brows and he hurried to clarify. "You chew a piece and, as long as it's in your mouth you blend into the surroundings, invisible."

That sounded promising. "Okay. I like the sound of that, but what if it fails. We don't know how the energy works here. My tracking magics are only half working."

Mandy shrugged, unzipping the bag and extracting a short stick of the green stuff, with leaves sticking out of it. "Only one way to find out." She popped the stick into her mouth and bit down. And shimmered out of sight.

Deg laughed softly. I gave him a cautious grin. "I'm still not sure…"

"Come on, LA!" The floating bag said. "This route will save us hours of walking. I don't know about you but I'm getting really tired."

I frowned at the bag. "You could be getting more rest than you want if those demons get hold of you. Like eternal rest."

The bag sighed, shimmering on the air.

"I agree with Mandy," Deg said. "We're in danger out here. We need to get to Trudy as quickly as we can."

The bag waited expectantly in mid-air. I glanced toward the pathway, still cloaked in oily evil, with a handful of skulking shapes arrayed along its length. Finally, I nodded. "Okay, but I want to go on record as being against this."

"Noted," said the bag. It opened a beat later and a stick like the one Mandy chowed floated toward Deg and another one toward me. The bag disappeared. I assumed Mandy had returned it to her pocket.

I watched Deg chomp down on his and disappear. I looked at mine, sniffed it, and frowned.

"Stop being such a baby, LA," the "Witch with a B" snarled.

I shook my head, determined that if her magic killed me I'd haunt her until she drooled.

"LA!" a disembodied "Witchy with a B" voice said.

"Hold your broom, Witch. I'm gearing up to this."

I ignored the sigh and then, closing my eyes and saying a quick prayer, I stuck the thing into my mouth. My fear was that it would taste like dirt. Or bird poop…not that I know what that tastes like. Or tree bark. What it actually tasted like was nothing.

Until I bit down on it to set the magic into motion.

Then it tasted like poop. I grimaced, gagging, and wondered how Mandy and Deg could chow down on theirs without throwing up. "Oh, stars that's awful." Why hadn't I thought to bring my *invisibilia* potion? Oh yeah, because I'd only had enough for one of us. Right at that moment I was thinking "every man for himself" sounded like a good motto.

"What…?" Deg said.

"Let's get going," Mandy cut him off and I heard the unmistakable sound of her swishing past me. That's when I realized the next problem. I couldn't see Deg and Mandy. I assumed they couldn't see me either. "How are we…" I gagged again as the stick rolled to the back of my tongue. I captured it with my teeth and determinedly held it there. "I can't see you. How are we going to keep from running into each other?"

Something warm in the shape of a hand found my arm and slid down to clasp my fingers. I recognized Deg's delicious sandalwood and wood smoke scent. "How's this?" He asked in a warm voice that was strangely sans gagging.

"That'll work, I choked out. How in the world can you stand…"

"Hurry up you two," came a harsh whisper from several

feet away. "We have a mean, pinching relative to find and a bunch of demons to evade."

I heard Deg sigh. "Remind me that I need at least a month away from her once we get back."

"Oh, I don't think I'll need to remind you. I'm pretty sure it'll be written in blood on both our foreheads by then."

## CHAPTER SIX

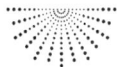

*W*e hadn't gone very far before the first challenge presented itself. One thing the nasty tasting sticks apparently couldn't control was scent. The monsters in the shadows could apparently still smell us. And if the taste of the stupid thing in my mouth was any indication, I'm sure we smelled like a freshly minted pile of feces.

I had no way of knowing where Mandy was. She was somewhere up ahead on the path when the shadows split and two demons stepped into the light, their glowing red eyes searching the night for us.

Deg pulled me to a stop as the first one stepped right in front of us, its wide, greasy black nostrils flaring and its gaze gliding unerringly toward where we stood.

My heart pounded against my chest, sounding loud enough to draw the monster right to me. I dug in my toes, on the edge of taking off running when a rock flew through the air and hit the second demon in the head with a resounding crack.

The thing opened a wide mouth filled with razor sharp

teeth and screamed, drawing the attention of the demon standing in front of Deg and me.

I didn't hesitate. Tugging Deg's hand, I shifted to the left of the demon and pulled Deg with me as I started to run.

Unfortunately, running was a bad idea. Our feet kicked up tiny clouds of black, silty dust, giving the demons a visual road map to follow.

The one on the path lifted off the ground, his huge wings pounding the air in reverberations so powerful they bent the flame on the burning bushes sideways. Deg and I picked up speed but we were never going to outrun a flying demon.

And at that point the demon Mandy had clocked with the rock surged into the air, apparently joining the pursuit.

At the last minute, Deg wrenched to a stop and dove toward the ground at the side of the path, taking me down with him. We hit a prickly brown bush of some kind, the densely tangled branches of which sliced through my flesh as I landed.

Before I could stop myself, I gave a small cry of pain. The nasty stick in my mouth fell out, disappearing inside the bush.

It took me a moment to realize what that meant. We were encompassed in darkness, deep inside the painful bush, and I stupidly thought I was safe.

To be honest, I was relieved to have the hated taste of the thing out of my mouth.

But then the ground shook beneath a couple of massive feet and hot breath, smelling of sulfur and death, sifted down on me.

I was afraid to look. My hand tightened around Deg's and he stirred slightly, as if he was looking up at the creature towering over us.

*Don't make a sound, LA*, he whispered through my mind, clearly shaken.

Deg shifted sideways, trying to pull me underneath him, but the branches of the bush trembled under his movement so he stilled.

A deep, moist breathing filled the night air, raspy and unhealthy sounding. The demon grunted softly, then coughed, sending foul smelling droplets over our hiding spot.

I grimaced as something landed on my arm.

Holding my breath, I prayed we were hidden well enough by the leafless tangle of bush that the demon wouldn't see me. Hot breath wafted over us again and the sound of rustling ensued as the demon moved closer. He was so close I could feel the heat from his oversized body.

It was like getting too close to a fire that was dying down but was still too hot.

Sweat ran down my face and between my shoulder blades and I tried not to breathe, fearing even the small movement of my chest rising and falling would give me away.

My first awareness that I was in deep trouble was a painful one. A claw found my throat, scraping a shallow but agonizing scratch beneath my chin.

The scrape stung like someone had poured salt into it and I had to bite back a scream. The area around the wound grew unnaturally hot, painting the entire side of my face and neck with sizzling pain.

An enormous, clawed hand wrapped around my throat and wrenched me off the ground. I barely had time to let go of Deg before the demon yanked me out of the bush and lifted me into the air with a joyful scream.

An answering scream joined the first, then another and another. I clasped the demon's thick, scaly forearms in an effort not to lose my head as he dragged me into the sky by the throat.

I couldn't pull air into my lungs. Though I struggled

mightily for a moment, the lack of air to my brain quickly took its toll. The world turned charcoal gray at the edges and bled inward, slowly closing off my vision.

All around us, the sky filled with black, flying shapes. I realized with horror that Deg hung from the claws of another demon and, in the distance, the strangely writhing form of a third demon probably meant he'd found Mandy. Though she still seemed to be holding tight to her magical little stick.

My eyes closed as weakness claimed me, and my muscles went limp.

Deg screamed my name. I twitched but couldn't find it within myself to look his way. Our mental connection flared briefly, his voice said my name, and then it went quiet.

I was afraid of what that meant.

Death called out to me and I was beyond fighting it. I gave up, let go, and waited for the pinprick of light behind my lids to blink out.

But it wasn't to be.

Light and sound burst upon the sulfurous night and blasted against me, warm and comforting. The demon that was holding me stiffened, screaming and writhing as if the beautiful illumination burned, and then let go of my throat.

I plunged downward, air rushing into my open mouth and filling my starved lungs. I coughed, my eyes coming open in sheer panic as I realized I'd escaped death by the demon's clawed hand, only to be bashed to pieces on the hard ground below.

I looked down, squinting against the brutally bright white light filling the entire area, and realized with a start that my descent was slowing.

My feet touched the ground and I stumbled, more from blindness and exhaustion than because I hit too hard.

I fell to my knees and half-covered my eyes, peering beneath my palm in an attempt to see the source of the light.

I thought I saw a small, humanoid shape at the center of the glow, not ten feet away. I tried to climb to my feet. There was no way to know if the creature standing so close was friend or foe. After what I'd just survived, I figured it was prudent to be careful.

Weakened by lack of oxygen and not a little fear, my traitorous muscles didn't want to cooperate. It seemed to take forever to get my feet underneath me and when I straightened, it felt like I was standing on a boat in the middle of a rolling sea.

I nearly fell back down and had to grab hold of a nearby skeleton of a tree.

The creature at the center of the glow lowered its arms and stood staring at me. From what I could see beyond the light stinging my eyes, the newcomer was small, child sized really, and appeared to have long, golden hair. The slender form was wreathed in shimmering robes that danced on a power-induced breeze.

Something shifted just behind it, the light glinting off the edges to blind me even more.

"Do you think you could tone that down a little?" a snotty voice said from not too far away.

Mandy was apparently safe…if a bit snarky.

"Oh. So sorry," said a childlike voice that I recognized. The light dimmed away, until all that was left was a gentle glow that highlighted a pretty young girl with a sweet smile. "Hello, LeeAnn," the girl said.

I almost fell to the ground. My mouth dropped open, probably very unattractively, and I gaped for a full minute, unable to respond.

"LA?" Deg moved close. "Are you okay?"

I reached out and clutched his arm, my fingers digging into it with something that felt like desperation.

The little girl frowned. "Have I done something wrong?"

I continued to stare at her for another minute and then realized I owed her a response. "Wrong? Maybe. Or not. Why didn't you tell me?"

She shook her head, the silky blonde curtain swinging around her face in perfect curls. "I couldn't. We've been under cover."

"We?" Then I realized. "The boys too?"

She nodded. "Ralph hated to fool you. He's generally very sweet."

*Deer*! Of course. I shook my head. "I can't believe it."

"Are you going to enlighten the rest of us?" Mandy asked, moving into the gentle radiance of the little girl's glow.

I looked at her and at Deg. His handsome face wore the first traces of understanding. "You won't believe it."

Deg smiled. "I think I will."

"Will somebody tell me what's going on?" Mandy said angrily. Patience wasn't one of her better things.

Silence throbbed between us for another beat. When I realized neither Deg nor the little girl were going to respond, I stared into the child's face and said. "Mandy, meet Mabel. Our helpful little kitten friend."

# CHAPTER SEVEN

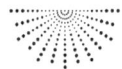

"So, what are you? An angel?" I asked Mabel.

"Nephilim, actually. Our father was an angel. Our mother was a Familiar."

A light bulb went off in my head. "Ah, that's why you can shift?"

Mabel nodded. "We were sent to the human dimension to keep an eye on things…to make sure Trudy doesn't make any inroads there."

I frowned. "But you're so young."

Mabel smiled, her pretty face growing pink. "I'm actually two hundred and twelve. Nephilim age very slowly."

"How long have you been watching us," Deg asked on a frown.

Mabel shrugged. "A decade, I think. Time is a construct we don't pay much attention to, I'm afraid."

"Okay, what's the play here?" Mandy asked. "I assume there's a reason you're here with us now."

"Yes. I've been watching over you. I wasn't supposed to step in but I couldn't just watch the demons extinguish you all." She frowned. "If only I'd gotten here soon enough to protect Brock."

A wave of sadness overcame me. We all stood in silence for a long moment, none of us willing to ask the question that would finalize his end.

Mabel's light began to fade. "We must move. The demons will be aware of the disturbance in their pathway. More will be coming."

"Can't you just blast them again?" Mandy asked with a crooked smile that didn't quite reach her eyes. I knew she and Brock were close. If he was dead...

I sliced that thought away before it could take hold. If I let myself think about Brock's demise, I'd be incapable of moving forward because of my grief.

"I don't know what your council told you but those of us who form the rebellion are on precarious ground here. We have only survived by keeping a very low profile. I'm afraid I've already done great damage by intervening in such a spectacular way."

We fell into step behind Mabel. She moved away from the lighted pathway, taking us into the deep darkness of the surrounding countryside. The Nephilim didn't exactly light our way, but her filmy white robes were like a beacon in the darkness, making it possible to follow where otherwise we'd be blind.

"At least I don't have to suck on that nasty stick anymore," I said to Deg. "It tasted horrible."

He frowned. "Really? Mine tasted like mint."

I stared at him for a moment and then scanned a scathing look toward Mandy. She grinned wickedly. "What? They're assorted flavors. Mine tasted like ice cream."

"Let me guess, I got the one that tasted like poop?"

Her eyes went wide. "I wouldn't know what poop tastes like, LA. I'm appalled that you do."

I glared at her for a moment before turning away in disgust.

She had to cover her lips with a hand in an attempt to hide her smile.

I'd been had.

And *that* is why I call her a "Witch with a B".

A LONG WHILE LATER, the ground beneath our feet started to feel boggy. Mabel warned us several times to walk exactly in her footsteps, not deviating even an inch. "If you fall off this narrow path you will sink beneath the surface of that black water and be lost."

I cast a terrified gaze toward the glossy blackness on either side of the path and fought an urge to grab hold of Mabel's robes and let her tow me safely to the other side.

Drowning was my greatest fear in life. Particularly when the liquid I'd be drowning in was inky with malevolence, with an oily surface that undulated constantly as if filled with writhing snakes.

My companions were silent, which told me they were as tense as I was about where we were. It didn't help that we could hear the strange cries of some kind of creature in the near distance, punctuated by an occasional shriek that made my skin crawl with fear.

Mabel stopped suddenly and I almost ran into her back. She threw up a hand, indicating we should wait. She'd done this a couple of times since we'd entered the bog, and after a moment she'd gone on.

I didn't know what she was tracking, but I was pretty sure I wouldn't like it if it found us.

My gaze slid briefly to the skyline and I was devastated to see that the glow in the sky hadn't moved any closer, despite the fact that it felt like we'd been traveling for hours. I was concerned that we wouldn't get to our destination before light started to peer over the horizon.

Then I realized I had no idea if that would even happen. We were in a whole different dimension, with possibly different world rules and realities I couldn't anticipate.

Morning might never come.

Mabel stood perfectly still before me. The moment stretched out, with only the roll and slap of the thick black water moving around our feet. I cast my gaze over the surface, squinting when the movement along its surface seemed to grow, the rolling liquid breaking higher from the surface than a moment earlier.

I was so focused on watching it that I forgot not to move. I shifted sideways, my foot slipping off the edge of the path and barely touching the black liquid.

I gave a little scream but a strong hand grasped my arm, yanking me upright before I could topple into the bog.

My heart thudding in my chest, I took a deep breath, closing my eyes and trying to calm my senses.

"Don't be such a klutz," Mandy whispered harshly.

I bit back a retort. After spending the last several weeks in her near constant presence, I was starting to understand the cranky Witch. She usually snapped when she was scared. Otherwise she relied mostly on snotty superiority and mean jokes.

Something splashed nearby and my eyes flew open.

Our gazes swung in the direction of the sound and Mabel sucked air in a gasp. "You've awoken it."

I frowned. "Awoken what?"

With a breathy roar that stunk of sulfur, the inky water rose straight up into the air in a long, slender column and, before we realized what was happening, fell toward the path, hitting it like an explosion and shaking the surface so hard we stumbled.

"Run!" Mabel screamed and took off, her feet barely touching the ground as she fairly flew along the narrow, twisting pathway.

Nobody had to tell me twice. I didn't know what I was running from but, after seeing an example of Mabel's power, if she was afraid of it, I was terrified.

Deg's heavy footsteps pounded along behind me, so close he clipped the back of my heels a couple of times. I realized I was holding him back.

That thought came home to me even more stridently when the black liquid rose up just behind him, towering over his head by easily ten feet, and then started downward.

It was going to smash into him and he'd go down, plunging into the terrifying bog.

"Deg, watch out!"

Not even taking the time to look back, he lifted a hand and screamed a power word, shortcut magic, sending a fiery arrow of energy into the thing descending on him. The energy severed the top four feet of the ebony column and it toppled sideways, hitting the path with a heavy splash and a roar that shook the pathway.

Deg cried out as some of it hit him in the back.

I didn't waste any time thinking about whether what I was going to do was smart. I just knew I had to do it. I yanked my magic forward and felt the shift take hold, ripping painfully through me as I gave the unaccustomed magic full rein. Leaping into the air, I writhed and screamed and came down on the other side of my shift as a cat. I bounded forward, three times faster than I could have run as a human.

I twisted my head backward and saw a lean, streamlined charcoal grey dog where Deg had been.

I almost fell off the path.

Another monstrous roar made my fur stand on end.

The pathway rumbled as the thing in the bog rose up again. It split into three massive columns that stunk of sulfur. The ominous protrusions crashed simultaneously onto the marshy path, ripping it into pieces behind us.

The path grew more narrow as we ran, to the point where I wasn't sure I'd have been able to stick to it if I'd been in my humanoid shape. I had a sudden, razor-sharp worry that it would stop before we reached the end of the bog.

Far ahead of us, Mabel suddenly disappeared. I almost screeched to a stop, surprise and panic swamping me.

Had she fallen in?

Only Deg's harsh panting and heavy paw-steps behind me spurred me on. Whatever was ahead I'd have to deal with it when I got there.

The thing in the bog was snaking along the pathway now, compressing the boggy ground with its weight and shaking it apart.

To my everlasting horror, the marshy earth started to tremble apart under our paws.

I bounded forward and nearly leapt right off the pathway before I realized that it had made a sharp turn. The curve was hidden by some kind of fold in the atmosphere. A deadly trick that probably cost many an unsuspecting traveler their lives.

I yowled as my paws stepped off the path, looking helplessly down at the roiling black liquid reaching for me.

Just before my paws touched the bog, Deg snatched me out of the air with his teeth and flung me none too gently back onto the path. I hit the relatively firm ground in a dead run, my shoulders screaming in pain from where his teeth had pierced my flesh.

After a few beats I spotted Mabel up ahead. She hadn't

fallen off after all. She must have known about the treacherous fold.

I silently thanked Deg for saving me. His quick reflexes had clearly saved my life.

Again.

We finally hit solid ground and ran several more yards before skidding to a panting stop.

We found Mabel resting against a tree, her face flushed and her robes still bunched in her small hands from when she'd been running.

Deg and I shifted quickly back.

The Nephilim handed us each a layer of her robes to cover up in and Deg winced as he eased his over his tall, spectacularly naked form.

Not that I noticed.

"What's wrong?" I asked him, moving quickly to his side.

"Nothing. I just got burned by some of that stuff. Mandy can heal me..." His head came up and his eyes went wide. "Mandy!"

We both looked back toward the ruined pathway and the bog, still roiling with agitation.

There was no Mandy.

She was gone.

# CHAPTER EIGHT

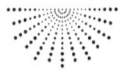

o say that our footsteps were heavy as we continued on, would be a vast understatement. Consumed by guilt, I'd tried to run back to find Mandy. Deg had barely been able to stop me. I couldn't believe she was gone. I'd lost two of my friends in the space of a few hours.

And Mandy's loss was all on me. If I hadn't accidentally touched the black liquid in the bog...

After Deg stopped me from going back, I'd collapsed alongside the black water and given in to the exhaustion riding me. But tears and desperate sobs only served to entrench me deeper into the cocoon of fear and loss I'd built for myself.

If Mabel and Deg hadn't hauled me to my feet, even scolding me about risking everybody's lives with my noise, I'd have probably thrown myself to the ground and indulged in an extended pity party for one.

As it was, I barely cared anymore if we were discovered. I felt so defeated, so worthless as a friend, that I could barely move.

Why hadn't I been able to help them? Why hadn't I been more careful with their lives. Why were they gone?

I drew a shuddering breath, fighting tears, and felt Deg's soothing energy washing over me.

*Stop beating yourself up, LA. None of this is your fault.*

I just shook my head, sniffling. I was too depressed even to share our mutual communication channel with him.

Ahead of us, Mabel suddenly stopped. She turned to us and put a finger over her lips, jerking her head toward a rocky area not too far away. "We have company," she whispered softly. "Hide."

I was halfway to the rock before I realized she wasn't coming with us. I turned with a small sound of alarm and started back. Deg grabbed my arm and dragged me behind a large rock. "She belongs here," he whispered. "We don't."

I understood what he was telling me, though I didn't like it one bit.

We crouched behind the landscape of big, black rocks and watched as the night shifted and puked three very large, man-like creatures out of it. They were well over six feet tall and wore armor crafted of blackened metal. The helmets they wore covered their heads from above the ears and were topped off with short horns that curved dangerously forward.

Mabel allowed her light to glow softly as they approached, her posture relaxed. She lifted her hands in greeting. "Hello. What are you doing out here tonight? Isn't the coronation about to begin?"

The soldiers stood in a triangle, the largest of them, whose armor was marked with a blood-red slash across the front, stood at the rear apex of the formation. He rested a long, spear-like weapon on the ground and leaned into it, cocking his head slightly. "More importantly, Nephilim, what are you doing out here. You aren't planning to disrupt the ceremony, are you?"

Mabel laughed, the sound pitched high and pleasantly musical. It sounded like a child's laugh, which I guessed it was. "Why would I do that. Has not Queen Trudy been good to my brothers and I? We have no complaints with her rule. And those who would work against her have tried, repeatedly to kill us. Does that not speak to our loyalty?"

The guard didn't say anything for a long moment, then he nodded, straightening and pounding the hilt of his spear on the hard ground three times.

I blinked at Deg. *Was that some kind of message?*

*Must be. I only hope he told them there was nothing to see here.*

Mabel's form tightened just enough for me to notice, because I was watching her carefully. *Not good*, I told Deg.

*Apparently not*, he agreed.

"We felt a large energy use in this sector. Was that you, Nephilim?"

Mabel nodded. "Demons attacked. I was alone and had no choice but to use a show of force." She stopped talking and waited for him to react. A smart move. Liars generally babbled on, creating details they didn't need because they were nervous.

Mabel was clearly an accomplished liar.

Although, technically, what she said was true. She'd just neglected to mention *us*.

Tension filled the air for a long moment as the guard stared at Mabel and she folded her hands and forced her shoulders to relax. I couldn't see her expression but I got the impression she was probably smiling.

Finally, the guard inclined his head. "Very well. Though the ceremony's been cancelled, we'll accompany you to *Mundala*."

To her credit, Mabel barely hesitated. She nodded,

moving swiftly toward the men and sliding between them to lead the way.

If her steps were a bit choppy, her posture slightly stiff, I hoped only I would notice. When the three guards were out of sight, I collapsed to my butt and leaned against the rock, expelling air. "Well, that was terrifying. Those guys didn't look any friendlier than the demons."

Deg's gaze still scoured the night, his expression tense. "I'm sure they're not. I wonder why the ceremony's been cancelled this time."

I pushed to my feet, brushing black dust off my jeans. "I guess we'd better follow them. As soon as we get a chance we'll have to spring Mabel."

Deg nodded. "She can lose herself in the assembled crowd once she gets there. I assume even if it's been cancelled there will be people there who'd expected to watch the ceremony. It should be easy to move around without being noticed."

We started walking quickly in the direction Mabel and the guards had gone. I was worried about being able to see them in the dark but Mabel had helpfully kept her glow and I could see the flush of it on the air ahead.

Unfortunately, we were so busy trying to follow Mabel we forgot to worry about what might be around us.

Big mistake.

The shadows in front of us shifted suddenly and I found myself with the razor-sharp point of a spear at my throat.

"Don't move."

I went very still as I felt the tip of the spear pinching against my skin. A slight burning sensation accompanied the sting of the blade and I smelled a whiff of something floral and not unpleasant.

"Devil's Bloom," a gravelly voice said from behind me. I rolled my eyes to the side as the guard with the red slash in his armor strolled into view. "A particularly horrible way to die. We coat all our blades in the stuff." He stopped in front of me, scanning a glance from my head to my toes and then back again. He barely skimmed Deg a look, dismissing him. That was good. It would hopefully prove to be a fatal mistake. "I don't recommend you give us cause to use it. I knew the Nephilim was hiding something." He jerked a head toward the darkness and Mabel stumbled into view, her hands bound and two of the huge guards bracketing her. Their spears formed a deadly arrow toward her heart.

She held my gaze for a long moment and then let her gaze drop to the ground. There had been some message there, but I wasn't sure I could interpret it.

*Don't speak, don't struggle. Just play along,* Deg told me on our private channel. Apparently, he was better at reading Nephilim-ese than I was. Or he was just winging it.

Either way, stalling for time seemed like the best move. Unfortunately, staying silent wasn't my forte. "I'm here to see Trudy."

The guard stiffened slightly, two furrows appearing between his cold eyes. "What business would you have with the queen?"

I had a brief moment of panic. The moment of truth was upon me. I was in a strange land, surrounded by weird and deadly creatures and mired in even deadlier politics. I had no idea whom I could trust or what allegiances anybody held. Telling him who I was could be the end of me and Deg.

But I really had no choice. I tipped my chin up, hoping I looked sure of myself. And maybe just a touch arrogant, like the niece of a queen would. "She's my aunt."

I thought he'd be surprised. Or at least skeptical. But he only scanned me another long look. "Yes. I see the resemblance." To my vast surprise, he inclined his head to the guard whose spear burned against my skin. The spear disappeared from my throat.

I had only a heartbeat in time to breathe my relief before the deadly blade was repositioned under Deg's chin.

"His fate is in your hands," the head guard told me. He didn't even bother to look at Deg as he proclaimed his sentence. "If you make one wrong move he dies first." He jerked his head toward Mabel. "She's next."

I slowly lifted my hands, terror slicing through me. What even constituted a wrong move to the creature threatening my friends? What if I accidentally crossed some invisible line and it cost them their lives? I decided I couldn't risk it. I had to win him over to my side before something I couldn't live with happened. "I'm not here to cause trouble," I told him with a stiff smile. "I just want to speak to my aunt about a possible spot in her court." Until the words slipped from between my lips, I hadn't known I would speak them.

Beside me, Deg stiffened. I could feel his censure thickening the air between us. I'd been instructed not to take sides. It had been the key thing my mother had drummed into us before she'd sent us on the mission into *Axismundi*. Lay low, take no sides, fact-finding mission only.

Well, I'd just thrown the proverbial demon bomb into that plan.

Still, my instincts were telling me it had been the right move. I just hoped my instincts weren't wrong.

He studied me for a long moment, his gaze hard. "And why would a Witch from the human dimension want a position in *Axismundi*?" He clearly didn't believe me.

On the positive side. He'd called me a Witch. That was interesting.

"Our council is in disarray. They trust no one and they're squabbling among themselves constantly. We're a heartbeat away from full rebellion by some and in danger of dictatorial control by others. I see the writing on the wall. Things are changing. And I want to be on the winning side of that change."

I swallowed hard as he continued to stare down at me. I had no idea if anything I was saying would ring true. No idea how much of our goings on the *Axismundi* creatures were aware of. I was pretty sure Trudy knew what the council members in our dimension were doing. But I was also fairly certain her soldiers wouldn't be privy to it.

In fact, I was counting on that.

After a very long moment he jerked his head toward Deg. "And him?"

I opened my mouth to speak but Deg beat me to it. He bowed slightly, wincing as the blade at his throat no doubt bit into his skin. "Deggart the Witch at your service. I'm tired of watching the council lording it over the lesser houses. I want to be part of the new order."

The guard's demeanor didn't change. But he did hold Deg's gaze for a moment. "And the Nephilim?"

"We paid her to help us cross *Axismundi*. She knows nothing of our plans and has given us no reason to doubt that she is one of Trudy's most loyal supporters."

I held my breath, praying that I hadn't just signed Mabel's death warrant.

The seconds ticked by, thick with tension, and the guard finally jerked his head toward the path. "I'll let the queen decide what to do with you."

A big hand shoved against my shoulder and I stumbled forward, keeping an eye on my friends as we moved quickly through the dark. I mumbled soothing chants, tempted to try out a couple of protection spells. But I remembered the guard stating he'd felt Mabel's use of magic and I couldn't risk it. *Axismundi* clearly functioned under a different set of rules. I didn't dare risk annoying the guards leading us to my aunt.

I was pretty sure, if I could just get us to Trudy we'd be safe. She might be cray-cray in a dangerously unbalanced way, but she was still my aunt.

I was counting on blood being thicker than political goals.

It was a dangerous path to follow. But it seemed the only one we had.

# CHAPTER NINE

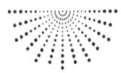

*T*rudy's "throne city" was nothing like I expected. It was beautiful, in a fairytale kind of way. But it appeared more an Elven glade than a Queen's castle.

The one thing I could appreciate, even in the dark, was the abundance of life.

The place teemed with it.

I smelled the greenery a quarter of a mile before I saw it.

And when I saw the vast horizon of trees and flowers, all sizes, shapes and colors, my first thought was to wonder how she'd created a living world inside a dead one. I felt no barrier holding the magic in when we crossed from the barren and ugly landscape we'd seen since arriving in *Axis-mundi*. No stench of sulfur.

But there was a sharp delineation between the two areas. And a shiny wall that rose into the sky and curved inward. It was like a giant bubble from a human child's bottle of liquid soap, stretching and popping around us as we pushed through. It closed behind us with a soft sigh, leaving behind only a sweet citrusy smell.

Lights flickered warmly as far as the eye could see in both directions. Glowing illumination wavered on a soft, flower-scented breeze, the blue flames perched atop heavily carved posts set into the ground at regular intervals along the border.

Deg scrutinized the carvings as we walked past, giving me a wide-eyed look meant to tell me there was trouble in them thar posts.

I'd noted the stiff slashes and awkward curves of demonic script. If Trudy was using magic to create her haven, it was of the black kind rather than the white energy I'd been taught since I was old enough to learn.

On its face, that seemed to be a bad indication of Trudy's character. But if she really wanted equality between the magic houses, she'd be inclined to utilize the skills and knowledge of all of them equally.

Unfortunately, that thought didn't make me any happier.

There were no roiling, noisy crowds as I'd expected. Only a few, fairly normal looking people walking to and from the various structures, which were built high in the trees, with plank and rope stairways leading to their rough timber doors.

Everyone was dressed in shimmering robes like Mabel's. In that moment, I realized she'd been dressed to fit in, rather than because she was part Angel.

I clutched my borrowed robe close, feeling exposed by the naked skin just beneath the shimmery fabric.

I had the strangest awareness of being different in Trudy's magicked world. It was more than having everyone stare at me. Though there was certainly a lot of staring going on. But it was more a feeling of being...heavy and inelegant...in a world filled with creatures who floated on air and shone silver against a gold background.

It was a totally unreasonable feeling, but I couldn't shake it, despite realizing it was probably some kind of warding or mind magic.

By the way Deg was frowning and continually shrugging his shoulders as if to slough off a weight of some kind, I figured he was feeling it too.

"Stop!"

I blinked in surprise at the head guard's growled command. I'd been so wrapped up in checking out my surroundings I'd forgotten how we'd come to be there.

The guard strode toward a sky-bound structure built on a copse of several massive trees. It was by far the largest and most beautiful structure in the place, with a roof of shiny-leafed tree branches covered in pink, blue and yellow flowers as big around as my hand. The wood slat walls were stained white and they were covered in flower-drenched vining. I realized with a start that the vines were formed in a protective warding design that surrounded the entire structure.

A wide walkway surrounded the structure, flowering vines twining around the railing as far as the eye could see. On the walkway, dozens of people sat and strolled, smiling and laughing and casting the occasional curious gaze our way.

Sour-faced guards stood at each of several doors in the structure's circular walls, pulling some of the lightness from the atmosphere with their dour defense.

Trudy's treehouse might not look like a traditional castle. But it certainly seemed to function like one. We waited several moments before the head guard reappeared at the top of the strange staircase to the castle. He lifted a hand and the guards shoved us, urging us forward. Climbing that wobbly staircase proved a skill that Deg and I didn't have. We fell to our knees several times before gaining the ability to shift with the movement instead of against it.

The guards chuckled as we fell again and again, never seeming to consider helping us. Mabel frowned back at us a few times and glared at the guards, but she was still bound and couldn't help us either.

Finally, we reached the relatively stable surface of the walkway. Yet even that moved slightly under our feet, giving the whole thing an unsettlingly insecure feeling I held onto until we entered through the widest set of doors.

Then I forgot the structure's stability. I forgot the guards prodding me with spears. I forgot I was on dangerous footing in more ways than one.

For a few beats I even forgot to breathe.

Because the room we entered was beyond anything I'd ever seen.

And the woman sitting in the enormous throne in the center of it, was celestial in her beauty.

The floor of the room was made of lush, vibrantly green grass. Filled with a golden light that mirrored the Earth's sun, the ceiling was higher above our heads than it had appeared from the outside. The sky reflected the gray-blue of the queen's eyes. Puffs of fluffy clouds moved lazily across the atmosphere and birds danced lazily on the air beneath them.

The room was decked out like a park, complete with a pond between the door where we stood and the queen's throne. A dainty bridge arched over the clear blue water and fish leapt from its glassy surface to snatch colorful dragon-flies from the air above it.

Around the room, people sat on benches and stood in clusters, speaking softly and laughing as if they hadn't a care in the world.

But despite the natural bounty of Trudy's "kingdom" the occasional hostile gaze still swept our way when our presence was noticed. And it took only a few beats before everyone stopped talking and turned to stare at us.

Expressions turned instantly hard. Smiles died on stiff lips. The sunny space and comfortably warm temperature soon turned cold under their scrutiny.

Trudy herself hadn't moved. Her impossibly beautiful face was formed in a stone-like mask, giving off no trace of warmth when her stormy blue gaze landed on me.

I hadn't been sure what to expect when I met my long-dead aunt. But hostile indifference had never been an outcome I would have predicted.

After a moment, she inclined her chin just slightly.

The guards shoved us forward and Deg and I shared a look. By mutual consent, we hadn't used our private communication channel since we'd been taken. We didn't know who could intercept our thoughts and if the guards would suspect its use.

I'd never missed our communication more than I did in that moment. I would have loved to hear Deg's impressions as we stepped off the dainty bridge and approached the throne.

Most importantly, I wasn't sure how to act in front of a woman who thought she was queen but really wasn't.

A woman who, by all accounts, was crazy as a loon and dangerous as a room filled with demons.

"Halt!" The head guard barked out the order when we were fifteen feet from the throne. He immediately dropped to one knee and lowered his head. "My Queen."

Deg touched my hand and gave it a surreptitious tug. We lowered our heads and stayed silent until she spoke.

"Hello, niece."

*Drop to one knee*, Deg's voice whispered in my head.

I somehow managed to lower myself without falling over, though I didn't do it half as gracefully as Deg.

"You may rise."

I might have been imagining things, but I thought Trudy's voice held a tinge of frustration. Though that made no sense at all.

She shifted slightly, her fingers tightening around a tall, polished staff she held in one hand. The staff had three leaves sticking up from the tip in a perfect circle, and the leaves danced constantly as if brushed by an errant breeze.

She handed the staff to a guard and motioned with her hand for me to approach. I moved slowly in her direction and, when she lifted her arms, bent to allow her to frame my face with her cool hands. She looked deep into my eyes, her expression not softening even a tiny bit. Trudy pinched both of my cheeks before giving me a tight smile. "You're so pale, child. You need color."

I'd winced at the cheek pinch but managed not to jerk away. "Part of being a redhead, I guess," I said softly.

Cocking her head, she finally let her eyes show some affection. "It's good to see you LeeAnn."

I gave her a smile. "It's good to see you too, Aunt..." I hesitated, frowning slightly. I wasn't sure what to call her.

"It's okay, child." She gave me a tight smile. "You may call me Auntie as you did when you were a tiny girl."

My frown deepened for a beat but I caught her clear gaze, seeing a warning written there. I nodded. "Thank you, Auntie. You're looking well."

*Well* was a vast understatement. She shared my mother, her sister's, red-gold curtain of glossy hair and beautiful eyes with a dense fan of lashes. Her facial features, also like my mother's, were delicate, arranged perfectly on her flawless, oval face.

She had a redhead's porcelain skin, without freckles to mar its unblemished surface.

The gown she wore was pale pink silk, cinched just below

her breasts in an old fashioned but flattering empire waist with several strings of creamy pearls. The gown hit her mid-calf and her slender feet were bare beneath the gown's hem. Strands of matching pearls encircled one ankle and the big toe on the opposite foot.

Her toenails were longish, filed square and polished to an opaline sheen, with a leaf that matched the ones on her staff painted on each big toe.

I hadn't lied. She looked the picture of comfort and health. But there was something in the tilted gray-blue gaze that made my chest tighten with dread.

"You look tired, niece." Trudy frowned. I was surprised when she stood up, wavering slightly and putting more weight than she should need to on the staff she'd retrieved from the guard. As she stood, the room fell as one to their knees, dropping their foreheads to the floor in front of them.

Trudy's eyes tightened with something that looked like irritation. She slammed her staff on the floor and everyone stood and moved quickly out of the room.

Finally, only the head guard stood before the throne. Trudy slid him a tense look. "Watch the doors."

He inclined his head. "With my life."

Something passed between them. I glanced at Deg to see if he'd noticed. He had. His mouth was a tight line.

The guard ascended the three steps to Trudy's throne and took her arm. She leaned heavily on him, her legs wobbly as they descended. I followed and, as they reached the grass, he handed her over to me. I took one arm and Deg moved in on her other side, ready to help if she needed it.

"We'll be in my rooms," Trudy told the guard.

He frowned, hesitating. "Are you sure, my…"

"Yes!" She cut him off with a glower and, though he clearly didn't approve, he bowed slightly and strode away, toward the doors we'd entered.

I realized suddenly that all the doors had been closed and I didn't doubt they were bolted. The feeling of foreboding I'd been struggling with deepened. Something wasn't right in Trudy's world.

Other than the fact that she was clearly ill.

# CHAPTER TEN

$\mathcal{W}$e moved around behind the dais and entered a door that lead to a long hallway. At the end of the hallway was a pair of gilded doors, thrown open to show a large area beyond that was filled with light. "My rooms," she told us with a tight smile.

By the time we reached the doors, Trudy was breathing heavily, her pale brow moist from the effort of walking the short distance.

The room was exactly what I would have expected. Lush, creamy carpets covered the floor of a massive area, whose main feature was a huge bed with polished tree trunks arcing toward the center from each corner. Gauzy pale green fabric was draped over the trunks and gathered in soft pools on every side.

The outside wall was mostly glass and beyond the window was a beautiful vista, featuring a waterfall at its center, whose base formed a pool that sparkled in the flickering light of a hundred lanterns set on carved posts like the ones we'd seen when we entered *Mundala*.

I got the impression we'd see massive trees and beds of flowers if the sun were shining.

"The divan, please." Trudy nearly gasped out the request.

Once we had her settled, I poured her a glass of a pink liquid from an icy metal pitcher. She took it, sipping gratefully. "Thank you, LeeAnn."

"Call me LA, please. Everyone does,"

Her smile was sad. "I've missed family. It's been far too long."

"You're not well?" I asked, hoping she didn't take offense.

She lowered the glass, staring at it for a moment. "No. I'm not."

"How can I help?" I realized I meant it and was shocked when the words emerged from my mouth. I'd thought I was coming to find a way to defeat a mad woman bent on destroying the world. Instead I found a sickly creature who seemed every bit as uncomfortable in *Axismundi* as I did.

It was probably all an act. But my heart was telling me I had to help. She was, after all, my family. I'd learned, not all that long ago, just how important family was, when I'd nearly lost all of mine.

She shook her head, settling back with a sigh and closing her eyes. "Just give me a moment." We waited in silence for a few seconds and then Trudy opened her eyes, lifting a hand and fluttering the long, pale fingers.

Harp music suddenly filled the room, its delicate notes dancing across the air like butterflies. It touched my skin in tiny electrical shocks and I flinched, realizing it was much more than music.

"Masking magic," Deg mumbled. He blinked in surprise. He'd probably not intended to speak the words out loud.

"Yes. I'm sorry for the intrigue, children. But I can't tell you how relieved I am to finally have you here."

I frowned. "Finally? Were you expecting us?"

"For some months now. I was unable to send a direct message of course, but I'd hoped your mother and grand-mother would catch the meaning behind the breach."

Deg and I shared a look. "The monsters were your doing?"

"Not directly, no. But, when I became aware of their infil-tration I didn't try to stop them." She pointed to a pile of clothing on a nearby chair. "Help yourselves. I'm sure you'll feel more comfortable."

As I dressed in jean cutoffs and a light blue tank top that fit me surprisingly well, I thought of the danger Deg and I had faced fighting the breach monsters and I frowned. "We could have been killed, Auntie."

She flipped a dismissive hand. "Clearly I have a better opinion of your abilities than you do. I doubt you and your handsome Witch were ever in any real danger. Besides, I happen to know the creatures were only on a scouting mission. They had no instruction to harm anyone."

"No instruction, maybe. But I assure you they tried really hard to harm us," Deg said angrily. He'd dressed in long jeans and a plain white tee shirt and looked much more comfortable.

Trudy shrugged. "I assure you that you were safe. Anyway, that's all in the past. You must listen carefully now because this is very important. In fact, it's dire. Your world is in terrible danger. In fact, all the worlds are being threatened."

She glanced toward Mabel and I realized, for the first time that the Nephilim hadn't spoken since entering the castle. "You and your brothers have done well, child."

Mabel pinched her gown between her fingers and curt-sied. "I live to serve, Majesty."

Trudy frowned. "You needn't continue the sham, child. We're alone."

Mabel glanced to her bound hands and the bindings fell away, falling to a pile on the lush carpets. "Ralph and Mack have already gone on to their destinations. I will go now that I have delivered LA and Deg to you."

I struggled to wrap my mind around what I was hearing. "You've been working together this whole time?"

Mabel inclined her head. "I am sorry for not being completely honest with you, LA. But it was necessary for you to remain ignorant of our plans."

"What plans?" Deg asked, his brows lowered in anger. "What have you involved us in?"

Trudy's gaze locked on his for a long moment and tension danced on the air between them. I fought an impulse to step in on Deg's behalf. Despite my worry that he might have overstepped, I realized he would need to earn Trudy's respect...and apparently her trust too.

Finally, she inclined her chin. "I understand that I have badly used you and for that you have my most heartfelt apology. But when you hear what I have to say I hope you will understand the secrecy. There are those in my kingdom who can pull thoughts from the minds of their enemies. I couldn't risk you having the wrong thought at the wrong time."

I shuddered. "I'm really glad I didn't know that before. It would have totally squigged me out."

Trudy stared blankly at me for a moment and then seemed to dismiss my statement as unworthy of more consideration. She took another sip from her glass. Color had returned to her pale cheeks and she seemed a bit livelier from her rest. "I want you to know that I would never knowingly harm you, child."

Her assurance sounded sincere but I wasn't sure if I could trust it. "Tell us what's going on."

She looked at Deg and, after the briefest hesitation, he nodded. He was willing to listen but from the frown on his handsome face I gathered there were no guarantees he would sign onto whatever Trudy had in mind.

"I admit I don't quite know where to begin." She pushed at the pillows behind her back and I hurried to help her sit up higher. "Thank you, LA."

She drank more of the pink liquid and then handed it to me. I settled it on the table and Deg and I lowered ourselves into a couple of dainty chairs.

Mabel dropped fluidly to the carpet, folding herself into a seated position with the flexibility of a child...or a magical creature. Her gowns spread around her like a shimmery puddle. She fixed a rapt expression on Trudy as if anxious to hear what Auntie had to say. Making me wonder why she didn't already know.

"I have an enemy in *Axismundi*. Someone who wants my throne." Her lovely mouth twisted slightly with distaste and I wondered at the cause. "As with any kingdom, *Mundala* has its intrigues. At first, I thought nothing of it. But my loyal friends have been reporting back to me with rumors that sounded all too plausible. Then I began to see the results of some of the intrigues set into practice. The breach into the human realm was a turning point for me. I realized I could no longer ignore the rumors. Someone intends to rip aside the barriers between all the dimensions and the chaos will be laid in my lap."

"Mother told us that was *your* plan," I objected softly.

"Yes, that is the rumor that's being spread. I assure you it isn't true."

Looking at her too-slender, slightly slumped form, I realized it would be too much of an undertaking for her in her present state. Unless she had a *lot* of help and stood to gain much from it.

As if reading my mind, Deg asked, "What is the goal of ripping down barriers between worlds?"

"Power of course. Once chaos explodes I will be removed forcibly from my throne. Most likely assassinated. And whomever is left standing with the strongest following will pick up the pieces and slide into power."

"You must have some idea who it is," I said. I couldn't believe Aunt Trudy would allow herself to be completely blindsided.

"I have my suspicions. But without proof they will buy me nothing."

"Who?" Deg demanded.

Trudy shook her head. "I won't cloud your judgement. I want you to have clear minds when you tackle this."

I frowned. "Say what?"

"I brought you here because of your previous skill in discovering the cause of the missing Familiars. You've proven yourselves adept at solving mysteries. I have a mystery I need solved. And we don't have much time. Whomever is plotting to destroy the barriers is moving forward very quickly."

I shook my head. "We just got lucky with the missing Familiar thing. We're hardly experienced investigators."

She leaned slightly forward, fixing an intense gaze on first me and then Deg. "But I *trust* you. That is the most important thing in this. I have only a handful of people I can trust. It is imperative that you do this for me."

Deg and I shared a look and a flood of unhappiness swamped me. "We didn't do it alone. Our friends were important in solving that case. And they're..." I couldn't bring myself to say the words. Deg reached out and squeezed my shoulder.

"Brock and Mandy didn't survive the trip here," Deg finished for me.

Trudy glanced at Mabel and the Nephilim rose, gliding

quickly from the room. "We have someone whom you can work with. I think you'll do well together."

I started to argue but decided against it. My friends had been difficult but I had grown to love and trust them each in my own way. I didn't have the energy...nor did we have the time it seemed...to develop that trust and love with new people.

But I couldn't bear to explain that to Trudy.

As it turned out, I didn't have the opportunity anyway.

The doors to Trudy's rooms burst open, slamming against the wall, and two lines of soldiers in full battle gear marched through. The guard with the red slash on his armor moved through the lines, his handsome face hard. His gaze sought Trudy and he gave her a long look before he stepped to the side and stood, hands clasped behind his back and staring blankly ahead.

Trudy barely reacted, in fact she settled back on her divan as if she'd been expecting the interruption.

The soldiers filed in and slipped sideways, creating an impenetrable wall between us and the door. A moment later they split apart in the center and a tall man walked through the breach. It slipped silently closed behind him.

He strode toward Trudy, barely offering us a glance, and gave her a cursory bow. The newcomer was handsome in a refined way, with sharp cheekbones and a wide brow and mouth. He had a thick mane of white hair that he wore in a man-bun at the top of his head and a piercing pale blue gaze. His nose was long and narrow, the nostrils flaring with irritation as Trudy met his gaze with a haughty one of her own. "Your Grace."

Trudy smiled coldly. "Reginald. What is the meaning of this?"

He pretended surprise. "I was told we had intruders. I came to remove them to the catacombs."

I might not have seen the tightening of the skin around her eyes if I hadn't been watching Trudy closely. It wasn't all that noticeable, really. Unless you were looking for it. What I didn't know was whether she was upset about his intrusion in her plans or about where he wanted to take us. I might be persnickety, but something called the catacombs didn't exactly sound like a day at the park.

"You overstep yourself, Reginald."

He skimmed a look my way, smiling meanly. The pale blue gaze was glacial. "I'm only doing my sworn duty, Your Grace. It is my job to keep you safe."

"I assure you, I'm perfectly safe. This is my niece from the human realm, come to be part of the new order."

His regard of me didn't warm even a smidgeon. In fact, as the icy gaze locked on mine, I read hostility in its depths, and suppressed a shudder. "I'm LeeAnn Mapes, sir. I've come to help my aunt with her plans for the new order. I assure you I'd never harm her. This is my friend Deg. He's here to help too."

Reginald addressed Trudy without acknowledging that I'd spoken. "All due respect, my Queen..." He all but sneered the address, clearly unhappy with her having the title.

I found that fascinating.

"...you have not spoken to this creature for decades. You have no idea what her intentions truly are. I have intelligence that lays the charge of spying at her feet." His lips curved with distaste as he glanced toward Deg. "Along with her travel companion."

Deg stood tall, his chin high. He returned the man's disdain tenfold. I nearly smiled. I'd been on the receiving end of Deg's stubborn streak and I knew for a fact it was nearly impermeable. The haughty Reginald would be disappointed if he hoped to intimidate the Witch.

"Who gave you that intelligence?" Trudy demanded.

Reginald shrugged narrow shoulders. "That is not important. I do not wish to reveal my informants." His smile was cruel. "For their own safety, of course."

His implication was clear. He was accusing Trudy of retribution.

"My niece and her companions are not spies," Trudy began.

"Companions?" Reginald asked, skimming a very deliberate glance around the room. "There are others?"

"My friends and I…" I started to explain.

Reginald ignored me. "If there are others they must be rounded up, Trudy."

"The others are…" Trudy glanced at me.

"They were killed on the way," Deg said in a cool tone. "Two lives lost trying to save the worlds. Almost immeasurable talent gone. And yet their loss apparently is going to be wasted, their reputations befouled."

To my horror, Reginald laughed. "I can assure you that nobody gives a rat demon's whiskers about their reputation or yours. When you practice villainy, the result is sometimes not to your liking."

Deg's hands fisted, his jaw turned to stone. I reached out and clutched his hand in silent warning. Until we knew what we were up against we had to keep our tempers in check.

A whisper of sound behind me drew my attention. I suddenly remembered the Nephilim. Why hadn't Reginald threatened her?

Glancing to the spot where she'd been sitting, I quickly saw why. She wasn't there.

I fought the ugly suspicion my mind had conjured. It wasn't possible that Mabel was Reginald's spy. Was it? Mabel was part of the world we found ourselves in. Her very survival depended on her staying out of the limelight. What if she had traded us to keep her own activities off Reginald's radar? She *had* mentioned going somewhere for Trudy. Her brothers had already left.

A flash of striped tail caught my eye near the door and I saw the tiny kitten slip past the guards unnoticed. She disappeared through the door, making her escape.

I hoped my suspicions about her were wrong. It wouldn't hurt to have someone on the outside who could help if the catacombs lived up to their formidable name.

"Take them!" Reginald suddenly barked.

I jumped, ripped from my thoughts as two of the guards grabbed me. Two others grabbed Deg. I willed him not to struggle. If we didn't cause any trouble they might put us both in the same cell. Then we could hopefully escape.

A cold, metal bracelet was slapped onto each of our wrists. To my surprise that was all the restraint they used. The bracelets weren't even attached.

Hope surged.

But Reginald quickly squelched it. "I wouldn't advise you try to use any magic." He jerked his head toward the bracelets. "You won't like what happens if you do."

"If you harm them, I swear you'll regret it," Trudy said.

Reginald shook his head. "You are being overly dramatic, as usual, Trudy." He jerked his head toward the door and the guards holding my arms jerked me forward.

I tried to glance toward my aunt but they shoved me roughly toward the door.

"It will be all right, LA," Trudy called out.

I would've loved to have believed her. If it weren't for the fact that she sounded terrified.

That didn't exactly give me the warm and fuzzies.

# CHAPTER ELEVEN

The catacombs were everything I feared and worse. We splashed through oily water that chilled and stained my feet in muck. The walls oozed a foul-smelling discharge that could have been rotted vegetation or some kind of oil. Judging by the slimy slickness on the rocky floor of the place, it was probably a mixture of both.

At some point Deg was yanked away, pulled down an unlit passage and disappearing from sight.

Deep throated screams of pain sliced through the icy cold, sounding muffled against the thick, gooey walls. Fear-filled bellows throbbed along the passageways and ripped at my nerves.

Something that didn't sound human screamed. All the hair on my body stood on end at the sound.

By the time the guards dragged me to a stop in front of a narrow, metal grate in the floor, my heart was beating so hard I saw stars.

I suddenly knew I couldn't go into that hole. The stench alone was like a fist to the nose. The total absence of light made my body shrink away.

I shook my head, trying to backtrack. "No, no, no, no…"

I hit an unmovable object and rough hands wrapped around my arms, squeezing painfully. "Don't cause me no trouble now, girl. I don't want ta hurt ye but I will."

The voice had the deep, gravel quality of a demon's and my terrified gaze shot to his. The eyes were black, not glowing, but I saw the curved tips of horns sticking out just above each ear.

"I can't go in there. I didn't do anything."

His smile was mean. His breath fetid. "I don't remember askin' ya if ya wanted it, girl."

There was a grinding screech of metal against metal and, before I knew what was happening, the guard gave me a hard shove.

I stumbled forward several steps, arms flailing, until my feet found air.

With a shriek of sheer terror, I fell into nothingness, and smashed hard into an unforgiving ground. The wet thwuck of slimy mud was a counterpoint to the painful thud of my flesh hitting the bottom of the hole.

As the guards slid the heavy grate back over the hole, I glanced up in terror. The opening was eight feet away. I realized I'd never be able to reach it. I slowly slid my gaze around the space, seeing only darkness. The only light was a small circle just beneath the hole above my head.

There could be something else in that pit with me and I'd never know it. The thought made my blood roar in my ears, and I felt suddenly dizzy. I lay very still, trying not to breath too hard for fear it would make me a target.

Forcing my mind to calm, I listened carefully to the darkness, trying to discern the tiniest movement or smallest soughing of air through lungs.

I didn't hear anybody…or anything…in the pit with me. But I had no way of knowing if that meant anything.

For all I knew there were creatures in *Axismundi* that didn't breathe and could lie perfectly still...stalking their prey with deadly focus.

I spent a few moments just pulling air into my lungs, focusing on a mental inventory of my working parts. I'd had the breath knocked out of me when I landed, and nausea threatened, both from the smack to my kidneys and the stench.

The smell was like a living force, crawling up my nostrils and into my mouth.

I pinched my lips closed and breathed shallowly, but that only made me feel like I was suffocating.

I had an almost uncontrollable desire to try to contact Deg through our mutual channel. But Reginald's warning rung in my ears. I didn't dare try using my magic until I knew what would happen. The thought made me remember the hardware on my wrists.

When I'd landed I'd sprawled, my arms out to my sides. They were covered in a couple inches of icy muck but I thought I saw a soft glow down near my hands.

Very slowly, I lifted one arm. The soft slurp of muck releasing my limb made me blink and go still.

Nothing came for me out of the darkness.

Nothing moved.

I finally decided I was alone and shoved to a seated position with a soft groan of pain. My whole body ached. I felt as if I'd been beaten with a baseball bat.

I stood up, wet mud falling off me with soft plopping sounds. Then the cold hit. My teeth began to chatter and I shivered so violently they clanked painfully together.

On the positive side, the bangles on my wrists gave off a soft light that I could use to see the space. I scraped as much muck as I could off of them and walked slowly around, illuminating the small area.

There wasn't much to see.

I guessed the circular room to be about ten feet across, with smooth, straight rock walls that offered no foothold for climbing.

The wall farthest from the opening had a two-foot-wide rock ledge at about knee height. The flat pad and rough looking blanket covering the ledge informed me of its purpose.

I stood in the center of the space, listening to the screams of the catacomb's inhabitants. The screams were accompanied by the clanking of grates and the rhythmic thud of something meaty hitting something hard.

The putrid stench made it hard to breathe. The bone-chilling cold made me want to curl up and pull the rough-looking blanket over my head.

I knew I needed to form a plan. I had to find a way out of my new cell and locate Deg. We had to get to Trudy and find out what she wanted us to do. I needed to...

My mind went blank. I stood there, seeing nothing as weariness dug its filthy claws into me and tugged, turning my knees to soft rubber.

Before I knew what I was doing, I'd dropped onto the crusty pad on the ledge and pulled the foul-smelling blanket over me.

I fell asleep with tears sliding from my eyes.

My mind shaping the faces of all the friends *Axismundi* had already ripped away from me.

A LOUD CLANGING noise woke me some time later. My eyes were swollen, scratchy, and glued shut from crying. I forced them open and, to my amazement, saw a small basket being lowered into the cell.

"Dinner!" growled a voice that sounded more animal than human.

I lay there a moment, staring at the small basket and wondering if I'd be able to eat. The aroma coming from inside was sour even beneath the stink of my horrible prison. I decided I didn't have the will to eat or the energy to get off my bunk and fetch it.

My eyes slid closed again and sleep tugged me near. My dreams had been chaotic and filled with uncertainty.

But as bad as they'd been. They were far preferable to the nightmare of the reality on the other side of my eyelids.

I don't know how long I lay on that hard bed.

My bones ached from the unforgiving surface and I shivered constantly with the cold. It was easier to sleep than it was to stay awake.

I lived in fear of the moment when I realized I couldn't sleep any more.

Because then I'd have to deal with the cell and everything it represented.

I had a vague recollection of three more baskets being lowered and, eventually, pulled back up.

Finally, my body screaming from inactivity and achiness, my eyes popped open and refused to close. I reluctantly shoved into an upright position and almost fell off onto the ground. Dizziness assailed me.

I slammed my hands to the wall and the ledge to keep from falling.

In the distance I heard the, now routine, clanging of grates and growled announcements. My stomach rumbled hungrily, despite a very real dread of what I'd find when I looked inside the little basket.

I'd have to eat something or I'd wither away and die in that terrible place. I suddenly realized I didn't want to die there.

I wanted to live.

But first I had to survive.

So, I waited for the opening of my grate with some anticipation. My stomach grumbling inconsolably and my mouth watering despite my reservations. When my time came I pushed forward on the bench, intending to snatch at the basket as it was lowered down.

I glanced up as the grate moved to the side and a dark, hairy face glared down at me, long, curved yellow teeth denting its lips from the top and the bottom. His ugly face curved into a terrible smile when he saw me. "Welcome back to the land of the sort of living," he growled. "You'll have five minutes to eat. Then I pull the basket back."

I dove on the basket as the grate dropped back into place.

I yanked a surprisingly pristine cloth off the top and started to reach inside. But the small mound in the center of the basket moved and I screamed, jumping back and slipping on the muck. My feet slid out from under me and I hit the slimy mess with a wet thwuck.

A tiny form jumped from the basket onto the ledge, landing lightly on dainty black paws.

"Mabel?"

The kitten's bright green gaze lifted to me and her tiny body shimmered, elongating and stretching into the young girl who'd led us to *Mundala*. "Hello, LA. How are you?"

I stared at her, unsure how to respond as she wrapped the rough blanket around her pale, slender form.

She blinked a few times. "Oh. Sorry." Mabel wiggled her fingers at the basket and a thick rectangle, tightly wrapped in clean paper, lifted from it and floated in my direction.

The savory scent of meat and freshly baked bread filled my sinuses.

"Real food?" I ripped the paper off and dove on the thick sandwich, moaning my delight. "This tastes amazing."

Mabel watched me eat with a soft smile. When I was finished she jerked her head toward the basket again. "Drink that and then it's time for us to go."

I swallowed my last bite and pulled a small flask from the basket. I sniffed it and was surprised that it smelled sweet and fruity. I downed the entire contents of the flask in one long pull, licking my lips when it was gone. "Delicious."

Mabel nodded. "That will give you energy. Are you ready?"

"I thought you'd never ask. How am I gonna get out of this hole?"

She pursed her lips and whistled. The grate slid sideways and a metal ladder clanked down, its feet slapping into the muck with a wet sound.

Mabel stood on the ledge, grimacing at the muck. "If you'd be so kind as to pull the basket up, I'll lead you through the tunnel that will take you out of here so you can continue your journey."

"Aren't you coming?"

She shook her golden head. "I have somewhere I need to be. I'm already two days late. It took me that long to find where they'd taken you and plan your rescue."

I wanted to hug her for that rescue, but having a cat's fastidiousness, I was pretty sure she wouldn't thank me for it. "I owe you my life."

"You owe Trudy. But I'm happy to do it. You don't deserve to be down here. Now we must hurry." She dropped the blanket and shivered, her form folding back down into the tiny kitten. She agilely leapt from the ledge to the basket.

I grabbed the rope and hurried to the ladder, climbing as quickly as my numb and unsteady legs would carry me. As my head popped through, I gently pushed the basket away from the opening and started to climb out.

A grimy hand appeared in front of my face. I looked up

into Deg's thin and filthy face. Despite his disreputable appearance, he was grinning widely.

He pulled me from the hole and I threw myself at him, nearly taking us both down to the ground. He stumbled backward, laughing softly.

"I was so worried," I told him as I scraped filthy curls away from his handsome face.

He looked into my eyes, emotion throbbing in his sexy quicksilver gaze. "I thought I'd never see you again." His gaze dropped to my mouth and our bodies drifted closer. I licked my lips, already tasting his kiss.

Pain sliced across my calf.

I yelped, looking down at the tiny black kitten, whose tail snapped angrily on the air.

Deg chuckled. "I think she's telling us to get moving."

I was happy to oblige. The sooner I could put distance between me and that horrible place, the better.

For the moment I didn't dwell on the challenges ahead.

It was all I could do to put one foot in front of the other through the murky madness of the *Axismundi* prison.

# CHAPTER TWELVE

*H*ours later, stumbling with cold and exhaustion, I finally saw a gentle, flickering light ahead, beyond a narrow opening in the rock.

Mabel cast a quick look back and then ducked through, disappearing from sight. I forced my frozen feet to move more quickly, stumbling and leaning heavily on the wall to keep from falling.

Behind me, Deg wasn't much better off. The days of cold and wet had taken their toll on us. We'd barely spoken two words since taking off down a narrow passage to escape the prison wing.

Since entering the passageway, we'd seen only a few guards moving between levels, climbing or descending the occasional ramp that rose into the darkness above our heads.

Mabel moved through the twisted maze of passages as if she'd been there before.

Many times.

I shuddered to think of the young Nephilim imprisoned there. It was certainly no place for a child. Even one of Angel birth.

I reached the sliver of an exit and plunged through, finding myself standing in a cave. Water trickled down the walls and pooled on the uneven rock floor.

Thunder rumbled in the distance, its power reverberating through my bones.

I felt like crying. We hadn't left the catacombs. I'd thought we were finally out of that horrible place. But I was still standing in water. I looked down, my feet raw from being wet for days. At least the puddle I currently stood in was warm.

In fact, I realized the air in the cave was warm too. And I suddenly understood what the distant thunder meant. I looked at Deg. "The waterfall!"

"It's close." We shared a relieved smile. He grabbed my hand and gave it a squeeze.

I frowned. "Where's Mabel?"

She wasn't in the small cave. There was no place to hide and there didn't appear to be any exits.

"Maybe there's a secret door…" Deg began patting the rock walls, looking for a hidden latch.

I joined him a minute later, fear making it hard to breathe. What if we'd hit a dead end? I couldn't turn around. I wouldn't go back to that prison.

I'd rather die.

A silvery glow suddenly showed behind one of the walls, and Mabel walked right through it. "Are you coming?"

"Did you just walk through that rock?" I asked.

She glanced at the wall, frowning. "Ah. You can't see past the cloaking." She reached out and stuck an arm through the rock. I could see the pale limb as if through gauze. She waved it around. "It's probably because of the bracelets."

Her words made me aware of a new problem. Or rather an old problem that suddenly seemed more pressing. "We need to get these off."

"We will. But first we need to get you to safety."

She disappeared through the wall again and Deg and I wasted no time following. The magic in the barrier nipped my skin as I passed through. It was an odd sensation… walking through what looked, to my blinded gaze, just as firm and solid as stone.

On the other side I turned back and the barrier was gone. I found myself looking into a three walled cave.

We were standing in yet another passage, but the air was hot and thick with moisture. A warm mist filtered over us and the thunder I'd heard before was a hundred times louder.

Mabel hurried forward. "Come. They'll be aware that you're gone by now and they'll be searching. We need to get through the waterfall."

Fear made my chest tight. With the catacombs far behind us, I'd been feeling as if we'd made it to safety. But her words reminded me we were still in danger.

Deg and I exchanged a glance and hurried after the Nephilim. A few short minutes later we emerged from the passage and found ourselves standing behind the waterfall.

The noise was impossibly loud. I stood in awe of the incredible power of the crashing water.

Mabel walked right into it and disappeared.

I took a deep breath, grabbed Deg's hand so we wouldn't get separated, and plunged into the falls behind her.

I'd expected to be pounded by falling water but something stopped it. The air above our heads shimmered iridescent. Frothy water slammed against the magic and rolled over without contacting us. I could smell the water, hear its roar, but not feel it against my skin.

It was not unlike the bubble encompassing Aunt Trudy's throne city.

Mabel was hurrying down a steep and narrow stairway cut into the stone on the face of the mountain. She stopped every few steps and turned a worried gaze our way, clearly concerned about being discovered.

My fear fed on hers and I found myself moving much too quickly for my tired legs down the narrow stairway. My foot slipped over the side and I was suddenly hanging out over open air, my stomach slamming up against my ribs. Deg's hand wrapped around my arm and jerked me back onto the steps. We crashed back against the wall and stood, my heart beating hard and fast against my ribs. "Thanks."

Deg nodded, his chest heaving. "We might want to slow down. I've almost missed a step or two myself. My legs are like rubber."

I nodded.

Mabel turned again and stopped, her hand coming up to point behind us. "Hurry!"

I looked where she was pointing and yelped in fear and surprise.

A massive creature with a craggy red face and huge, curved horns was running agilely down the steps toward us. He was so huge that it was strange to see him running so easily, but I realized if we didn't start moving again he'd be on us in a heartbeat.

So much for slowing down.

I took off running, tugging Deg along behind me as we tried to put distance between us and the demonic creature that was closing in fast.

Mabel was screaming something but I couldn't make it out in the noise of the waterfall. As we left the magic bubble behind, the real sound of rushing water finally filled the air.

When I looked again Mabel was running back up the steps, her pretty face filled with alarm. She was waving her arms, pointing behind us and still screaming.

I turned my head and shrieked, though the sound was swallowed by the roar of the falls.

A massive hand, fingers tipped with one inch long curved black claws, was hovering just behind Deg's shoulder.

Without thinking, I threw up a hand and flung a power word at the demon.

Fire burst from my hand and flared into an explosion that blew me right off the steps. Deg blasted off with me, arms flailing on the fiery air as flames licked hungrily at his skin.

I screamed in agony as flame burned my flesh, its touch a white-hot wall of unending pain. I could feel my skin melting under its touch...smell my hair burning...and underneath it all, was a slicing agony of blades fileting my internal organs into mush.

I hit something that felt like rock. Water shot into the air in a glistening wave and bubbles danced against my skin as all the air I held in my lungs filtered out into the cool, clear pool.

Sound crashed back, hitting my ear drums like a sonic boom that left me screeching in pain.

A heavy object hurtled into the water not too far away and, a beat later, something even bigger hit, sending ripples outward to shove me sideways in the pool.

I was disoriented for a moment, not knowing which way was up and which was down.

It wasn't until I hit the white sand at the bottom of the clear pool that I realized I was going to drown. My lungs burned with the need for air. It was all I could do to keep from opening my mouth and taking a deadly breath.

In desperation, I got my feet under me and shoved off, passing Deg on the way up. He was limp and his eyes were closed. He was sinking fast. If I didn't help him he'd die. Grabbing his hand, I kicked hard against the roiling white water, aiming for the edge, away from the constant clash of the falling water.

He was dead weight, pulling me down like an anchor.

I didn't want to release him for fear he'd be lost to me forever. But if I didn't get some air we would both die in that pool.

With a heavy heart, I forced my fingers to release his arm and shot toward the surface.

Bursting free of the water, I sucked in great gasping lungsful of air. I looked quickly around, but I didn't see Mabel.

I really needed her help getting Deg out of that roiling pool.

But she was nowhere to be seen. And, as I dragged as much air as I could into my lungs in preparation for another attempt at Deg, I realized we were out of time.

A great, dark, horned shape was streaming toward Deg's sprawled form at the bottom of the pool.

I screamed for Mabel and dove, spearing straight toward Deg's unmoving form. I had no idea what I was going to do when I met the demon underwater...I'd been so weak I was unable to help Deg get to the surface...but I had to do something.

When he spotted me coming, the demon's terrifying face opened up in a wide grin. I panicked, briefly reconsidering my choices.

Stupid choices. Stupid.

My mind raced. There had to be something to do. But I was magic-restrained and physically debilitated. And Deg was...

I swallowed hard, looking at his unmoving body at the bottom of the pool. He looked peaceful, like he was asleep.

But he wasn't asleep. And it was that stark reminder that forced me to do the unthinkable. I lifted a hand, my gaze locked onto the demon, and a power word throbbing on the back of my tongue.

The demon's eyes went wide. He started to shake his

head, his huge form slicing sideways, one arm outstretched to stop me.

But I had to save Deg. So, I screamed the power word into the watery cocoon.

*Expulsio!*

I'd thought the explosion on the mountainside had been violent. When the energy boomed away from me the second time, turning the very water encompassing us to pure fire, I was blown backward, flung out of the pool and sent screeching in agony, in an arcing flight through the moist, heated air beside the pool.

I hit the grassy area surrounding the water and skidded several feet, slamming up against a rocky outcropping and folding into a puddle at its base.

Knives sliced through my insides, slashing in rolling waves of pain that kept me screaming and thrashing in my mind.

Only in my mind.

Because my body couldn't move. I lay there, twitching violently as my insides were ripped to shreds. But my limbs seemed disconnected from my brain and they lay useless in the wet grass.

After what seemed like hours, the pain finally started to recede. I lay there, senseless with relief, and panting from the residual pain memory. It took me a moment to remember why I'd tested the stupid bangles on my wrists again.

I shoved to a sitting position. My gaze slipped hopefully around the area and I saw the demon, pushing to his knees on a groan.

The thing had survived. Freakin' fantastic!

I found Deg lying half inside the pool, several feet away. I didn't trust my legs to hold me so I got to my hands and knees and crawled as quickly as I could to his side.

He was icy cold, his skin blue, but he was twitching from the electrical blast of the magic kickback.

I'd jump started his heart!

Not my intended result but better. I'd only hoped to blast him out of the pool. I grabbed his shoulders and shook him, casting quick glances toward the enraged demon stalking our way. "Deg! Wake up, hurry..."

A silvery light appeared on the air between us and the demon and I sucked air in a surprised gasp. Mabel had finally arrived. And she stood between us and certain death. We were safe for the moment.

But I needed to get Deg out of there. If Mabel used her magic to hold the monster off, we'd be found. "Deg, come on, you need to wake up."

His eyes fluttered and slowly opened. Immediately, he started retching, regurgitating what looked like a couple of gallons of water onto the grass.

Deg groaned, wiping a hand over his mouth. "What train was I hit with that time?" He shook his head, turning a pain-filled glare my way. "Are you having trouble with the whole 'don't use your magic while wearing the bracelets' thing?"

"Shut up. I saved your life." I bristled slightly but his complaining was actually comforting. At least he was alive.

I was dimly aware of Mabel speaking to the demon, but I was focused on helping Deg to his feet and mostly tuned them out.

Imagine my surprise when I finally had him upright, leaning heavily on me, and turned to find the Nephilim and the demon standing side by side, glaring at us.

"Are you trying to kill me?" the demon asked in a tooth-filled snarl.

I blinked. "Well, yeah. If that's what it takes."

Mabel snorted. I gave her a disbelieving look as she smiled.

"LA, Deg, this is Abdiel. He works in the catacombs."

Deg took a step closer, his hands clenching into fists. "Worked…past tense…because I'm about to kill him."

The demon snorted, rolling his round, black eyes. "Pipe down, Witch. I'm on your side."

Deg's aura started to shimmer with silvery light and I grabbed his wrist. "Don't!"

Not only did none of us need another fiery explosion, but I was watching Mabel's body language. She wasn't afraid of Abdiel. "Is this true?"

She nodded. "Abdiel is loyal to Trudy. When he found out who you were he offered to help."

"Then why were you screaming at us to run from him?" I asked, totally confused.

"I wasn't. I saw him coming and realized how you'd take it. I was afraid you'd do exactly what you did. Although, I have to admit the outcome surprises me. Usually someone who uses magic while wearing Reginald's bracelets ends up in pieces."

Shoving that information away to examine later, I skimmed a look toward the demon. "What's going on? Who's Reginald and how is it possible he's able to roll right over Trudy like he did?"

The demon ran a long, black tongue over his lips, the tip slipping just behind the curved fangs. I barely restrained a shudder. "That's too long of a story for right now. But the *CliffsNotes* version is…"

I held up a hand. "Wait…you know about *CliffsNotes*?"

He rolled his eyes again. Apparently, the demon was sensitive *and* judgmental. "Of course. I don't live under a rock."

I looked at Mabel, shaking my head.

She grinned. "The demonic realm runs closely to the human realm. The two are actually very much alike."

Now *that* was a subject for another day. "Anyway," I said, returning my attention to the demon. "Give me the abbreviated version."

"Trudy didn't exactly ask to be queen. She was drafted by Reginald. It didn't take long for her to realize she was nothing more than a figurehead. Reginald is the force behind the throne."

Deg frowned. "Then why didn't he just become the ruler?"

"Because it would never be allowed," Mabel interjected. "Reginald comes from a long line of wizards, known to be cruel and motivated by their own interests alone. He has neither the bloodline nor the temperament to be king."

"So why does Trudy allow him to control her?" Deg asked. "If she's anything like LA and her mother and grandmother, she's no shrinking violet."

I spared him a smile. "That's true. From everything I've heard about my aunt, she was a powerful Familiar, more powerful than any of the rest of the women in our family. She wouldn't allow Reginald to control her unless..." My eyes went wide as I realized the truth. "He's poisoned her somehow, hasn't he? Weakened her to the point where she couldn't foment so much as a disagreement, let alone a rebellion."

Abdiel nodded. "He's using wizard magics on her. They keep her weak and slightly disoriented. It's actually a wonder she functions as well as she does under them. It's a testament to her power. Reginald expected her to be bedridden."

"Is there nobody who can help her?"

"Yes," Abdiel and Mabel said, almost in unison. "You."

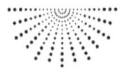

# CHAPTER THIRTEEN

"*M*e?" I questioned, shocked. "How?"

"Reginald has factions at all of the barriers between the dimensions. His plan is to blow the barriers with interdimensional breach bombs and overrun the other worlds. Once he has control of everything, he'll finish Trudy off and take the throne himself."

"That's why your brothers left," Deg mused.

"Yes. Each of them is in charge of one of the barriers. I must go to mine, which is between *Axismundi* and the demonic realm." She glanced at Abdiel, whose wide mouth had pinched around his fangs. "Abdiel has agreed to stay and help you free Trudy."

"How?" I asked. "We can't use magic and we have no idea who's with Trudy and who's against her."

"That's where my help is needed," Abdiel growled. He was clearly not happy about it.

Deg lifted his hands. "We're not going to be able to do much with these things on. No offense LA but I could do without your 'help' as long as you're wearing them."

I shook my head. "Ungrateful Witch."

"You almost killed me!"

"Yeah, but then I saved you again." I shrugged. In my mind we were pretty much even. Sort of.

"Almost killing me again in the process." Shaking his head, Deg glared at the demon. "Unless you know how to remove them?"

Abdiel's hand came up and I jerked backward, eyeing the deadly curved claws. He gave me a look. "If you'll allow me. I'm one of the bracelet keepers. I can remove them."

Looking to Mabel for reassurance that I could trust him, I slowly lifted my arms at her nod.

The demon reached out and touched a clawed fingertip to a bracelet, inserting the tip into a tiny hole I hadn't noticed before. The bracelet snicked open and fell to the ground at my feet. He quickly dispatched the other one and, after receiving a warning glare from Deg, removed his too.

We rubbed our raw and bloody wrists. "Those things are diabolical."

Abdiel's eyes narrowed. "Reginald isn't afraid to use torture to get what he wants. The catacombs were his idea too."

I shuddered.

"I don't have to tell you that we can't allow him to gain control of all of the dimensions," Mabel said.

"Not quite all," Abdiel reminded her.

She sighed. "We're not sure about that though, are we?"

"What do you mean?" I asked.

"The Heavenly dimension should be immune to his power. The gates have withstood all kinds of attacks over the millennia. They absorb the energy from each attempt and become immune to it for the next time. Wizards attempted to breach it three thousand years ago."

"Then it should be safe," Deg posited.

But Mabel didn't look convinced.

"What aren't you telling us?" I asked.

She sighed. "Reginald is part Dark Faery. It's the reason his power is so great and his magic so nasty. The Dark Faeries have never tried to breach the Heavenly barrier..."

"So, it might be enough to turn his wizard magic into a viable weapon," I finished for her.

We all stood in silence for a moment. Then Mabel's head came up. "But it won't be a concern because we're going to stop him." She gave us a sad smile. "I must go."

Abdiel's head swiveled, his black gaze going wide. "They come. We need to move."

Mabel touched Abdiel's arm. "Keep them safe my friend. And I promise to protect your people."

He inclined his head. "I'll hold you to that promise, little Nephilim."

As Mabel dissolved in a soft burst of light, Abdiel pointed to the falls. "Behind the falls there are passageways..."

My head was shaking before he finished the sentence. "I'm not going back inside that mountain."

He shook his head. "We don't have time to argue. In about ten seconds they're going to round that bend in the road and see us."

Deg grabbed my hand. "Come on, LA. If he tries to take us back to that hell hole you have my word I'll help you blast him to dust."

I skimmed the demon a glower.

He simply shook his head. "Move it!"

We started running, the demon striding quickly behind us. He hadn't been lying. We'd barely ducked beneath the thick wall of pounding water and spray before a large contingent of Reginald's soldiers rounded the bend.

We found a spot where we could watch them at the edge of the falls, obscured by the rising mist where the water hit the pond.

They stopped near where we'd been standing, one of the guards crouching down and picking up our discarded bracelets. They conferred for a moment and then one of them pointed toward the falls, the three in front gesturing wildly. They seemed to be arguing about something.

"What are they doing?" I asked Abdiel.

He sighed. "This area is protected by light magic. Trudy's followers were able to ward it off before Reginald got full control. It's the last bastion of positive energy in the place."

Something in the tone of his voice made me glance his way.

The demon's red face had gone pale. He was shaking and his skin was oily with sweat. His craggy lips were pinched around his fangs.

"What's wrong?"

He lifted his hands. "I'm stained from my exposure to Reginald. The warding is trying to expel me."

He dropped to one knee and leaned over, panting around a low groan. "It's like acid sliding over my skin."

The guards suddenly broke into movement, heading directly toward the pool.

I looked at Abdiel. "They're coming. What should we do?"

He shook his head, dropping down to the other knee and doubling over in obvious pain. "They...won't...come... inside..." He broke off, his jaw tight and his breath coming out in ragged moans.

Reginald's soldiers stopped at the spot where Deg, Abdiel and I had landed when I'd blasted us from the pool. The grass was mashed and mangled there.

I watched in horror as their gazes slid toward the waterfall. "They know we're in here."

Abdiel gave off a long, groan and fell to his side, writhing on the rocky ground.

"We need to keep him quiet," Deg said. He placed a hand over the demon's head and silvery light suddenly bathed it.

Abdiel cried out.

The soldiers' gazes shot toward the exact spot where we hid. One of them started moving. He certainly looked like he intended to come inside. He was mere yards from the edge of the falls when I panicked. He was showing no signs of being affected by the warding.

"He's coming in!" I told Deg.

Deg's head came up. "Shift!" he whispered harshly.

I didn't hesitate. I immediately grabbed my shifting energy and yanked it forward. Running toward a small gap in the cave wall, I leapt toward it just as I heard heavy foot-steps on the rocky floor. The world slanted, reshaped itself and turned gray and black. My feet hit the floor just inside the opening, landing with a soft plop I doubted anyone beyond the gap would hear.

I dug in and ran, my feline form low and fast in the small passage. Scents I hadn't noticed before assailed me. Sounds exploded in my sensitive ears.

The soft plop of heavy paws behind me stayed close and the sough of breath on the air was a steady, comforting song.

Deg was right behind me in his canine form.

We reached a turn in the passage and I screeched to a stop, panting with fear as the walls seemed to close in on me. I tried to breathe through the sudden panic, not sure what had initiated it.

Flashbacks of my days in the catacomb cell made my fur stand on end. I hissed softly as pain twisted in my belly.

Deg dropped to his haunches and looked at me, his sleek Greyhound form, much larger than mine, seemed to strain the boundaries of the passageway. If anyone should be feeling claustrophobic it was him.

But he seemed calm. His golden-brown gaze settled on

mine and a warmth infused me, coating the panic with a muffling energy.

He'd used our common energy pathway to send me calming magics. It was something we'd only recently discovered we could do.

*Thanks*, I told him tentatively.

By mutual, silent consent, we went very still, listening to the voices growling back and forth from the cave.

"What are you doing here, Abdiel?" A gruff voice asked.

"I...I thought I saw the escaped prisoners come in here."

"Are you stupid? You don't have my special protections. You must be in agony."

"I've had better days. A little help would be appreciated."

"Reginald will want a report. No one else has set eyes on them."

The inference was clear. Abdiel was going to be grilled. He might be locked in the catacombs. Because he'd helped us.

I felt bad for the demon but he clearly had known what he was signing up for when he'd volunteered to help. I'd ask Mabel about helping him later. Right at that moment we needed to get someplace where we could return to our human forms.

Deg climbed to his paws and gave me a long look, then he started forward, plodding down the passage that would lead us deeper into the mountain.

I bounded after Deg. The only way out of the current mess we were in was through it. At least we were finally moving under our own steam.

Eventually the passageway began widening. Ahead of us, the route was growing lighter, hopefully indicating an open cavern. Figuring it was probably flooded with the light of some kind of moon or stars, I didn't get overly excited.

I realized Deg was getting ahead of me and hurried my steps. In his canine form he was fast and agile and his legs were five times longer than mine. I made a mental note to test my shifting magic. Maybe I could shift into something with longer legs next time.

The thought made me smile.

The passage continued to brighten as we moved through it. My sensitive feline perception gathered information as we ran.

Fresh air, filled with the scent of flowers and growing things infused the musty stench of the passage. I could also smell the characteristic musk of a variety of wildlife. Smoke. And water.

My tongue came out to scrape across my dry lips at the thought. I was dehydrated after my time in the catacombs.

I shook off the thought and concentrated again on gathering information. The dead echoes of our paw-steps in the passage had been a constant since starting off. But ahead I heard sounds that indicated openness. There was a roar, the sound of water falling, and I had a sudden fear that we'd circled around and were back inside the catacombs.

Behind the roar of water, birds were singing. There were no birds in the catacombs. And the air was much cleaner than in that horrible place.

I honed my hearing to move past the roaring water.

I heard the scrape of something over rock.

A small creature rustled softly through the brush.

And someone spoke...

My pulse shot up. Almost at the same time, Deg and I slammed to a halt.

We crept slowly forward, keeping close to the walls. The air grew increasingly warmer and moist. The rock beneath our feet grew slick with moisture.

Just as before, the smell of the water drew us forward and, as we stepped into a small cavern that was much too similar to the one in Trudy's garden, we found ourselves looking at a shimmering wall of water, falling with a power and an energy that drove deep into my chest, echoing the beat of my heart.

Deg and I shared a look. By unspoken agreement we shifted back and moved to a spot just inside a rough-hewn opening in the rock.

We waited, listening, for evidence that people were near. And when we heard no one we stepped behind the roaring curtain of water.

We stood on the slick ledge and stared out at an incredible sight. A park, baking in the heat of a bright sun that hung in a cerulean blue sky.

In the distance was a recognizable pond. People sat at tables and lay on blankets in the shade.

Children played with toy boats in the water.

I turned an incredulous gaze toward Deg. His brow was knit in a frown. "It can't be," I told him.

He shook his head. "There's only one way to find out."

He stepped forward and I heard the taut ping of a magical barrier being breached. I pulled air into my lungs and followed him out from under the falls. The electricity of the energy barrier stung me briefly, like static electricity dancing over my skin as I pushed through.

Then I was standing in a blinding sun looking out over *Illusory Park*. The forest stood sentinel over the spot around us, its well-known scents and smells like balm to my jangled nerves.

Deg bent down and picked up a pile of clothing, showing me a shirt and jeans. "Is it possible someone knew we were coming?"

I took the clothes from him and pulled them on. He did the same.

We'd barely buttoned up before someone called our

names. My head jerked up and a smile formed on my lips. "Is this a trick?"

Deg gave a short bark of laughter. "If it is we're both being fooled. I see them too."

I took off running, shrieking with laughter, and slammed into Brock's arms, squeezing him tightly as Deg grabbed Mandy and swung her around.

I pulled back and cupped the demon's handsome face with my hands. "How? When? Nothing makes sense."

He nodded, his face uncharacteristically serious. "I'll explain later. We've been waiting for you. We need to go to *Familiar, Inc.*"

I knew by the tone of his voice that something wasn't right. "What is it? Is it mother?"

Mandy pulled me into a hug, and that alone was enough to make me worry. "It's not your mother. It's..." She glanced at Brock.

He frowned. "It's Celeste, LA. She's really sick. We were afraid she wouldn't make it until you got home."

# CHAPTER FOURTEEN

My mother's face was pinched when I walked into the room. She stood up from the hard wooden chair she was sitting in and walked over, wrapping her arms around me in a hug filled with as much desperation as love.

"How is she?" I asked.

Mother pulled away, glancing toward the bed, and sniffed, shaking her head. "I'm glad you got here in time."

My heart broke in two pieces and my knees buckled. I just couldn't believe the woman who'd raised me with a determined kind of strength and pride could be facing death.

It seemed so sudden.

"What happened? She'd been getting better."

Grandmama Celeste had suffered at the hands of a devious Familiar with uncommon powers and it had sucked a lot of the enduring magic out of her. She'd been tired and had aged from the event, but she'd been gaining strength in recent days and we all thought she'd soon be back to herself.

Mother squeezed my hand and turned toward the door. "I'll be right outside if you need me."

As the door closed behind my mother, my gaze slid to grandmama's bed. She barely made a lump in the covers.

Moving closer, I looked down on the too pale face, which was lined and gray with age. Tears flooded my eyes. Grandmama's frail form shivered beneath the tears and I scraped them angrily off my cheeks. "It's not fair," I said to no one in particular.

Grandmama's lids fluttered and opened. Seeing me, she smiled, reaching a bony hand to clasp mine. "Hello, LA. Did you complete your mission?"

I wasn't surprised Celeste knew about my super-secret mission. She would have been the only one mother told. I shook my head. "I'm afraid it's more complicated than we thought."

Grandmama sighed. "Of course it is, dear. Whenever Trudy's involved things are complicated." Her smile was shaky. "She just can't help herself, I'm afraid."

I struggled with whether to tell her that her youngest daughter was sick and at the mercy of a ruthlessly evil creature.

"What is it, LA?"

I bit back a sigh. She always could read me like a kindergarten primer. "Trudy's not in charge of the plot to merge the dimensions. She's being…controlled by someone."

Grandmama's red-rimmed blue-green eyes widened. "Is she? Well, that's quite a turn of events for her. She's always been one to try to control those around her. If she'd only been more humble, she'd probably still be with us today and leading *Familiar, Inc.*"

"Really? What happened to her? Why is she in *Axismundi?*"

Celeste patted my hand. "That's a long story for another time."

I bit back the plea that rose to my lips. There might not be another time. And I really wanted to understand what was happening.

Likely reading the disappointment in my face, Grandmama relented. "There are two ways to enter *Axismundi*. One is death. That buys you a spot in the Elysian Fields if you're lucky. Hades if you aren't." She paused for a beat, her gaze going soft as if considering what she had ahead of her.

"And the other?" I asked.

"Banishment," Celeste said softly. Her gaze sharpened on me. "Trudy was banished for trying to undermine the council."

I frowned.

She sighed. "I know that sounds like a minor thing, but our world functions on the razor's edge of control. We're the only dimension where creatures from warring and competing factions live together among humans. Humans are fragile and must be protected from our interference and machinations." She shook her head. "If our ruling body is usurped, all could explode into chaos. We can't allow that."

"That's why we have the web?" I asked. The web was a kind of magical Internet that tracked the whereabouts and energy use of every magical creature in the human dimension. It was the thing the rogue Familiar had been trying to hijack when Celeste was drained of her energy.

"Yes. It keeps us all honest. And its loss would be catastrophic."

"Celeste…" Tears burned in my eyes.

She patted my hand again. "Don't cry for me, LA. We all have our purpose and I must fulfill mine." She smiled gently. "We'll see each other again. You've learned of the special door to *Axismundi*?" She lifted her eyebrows in question.

"In the primordial forest. You could have knocked me over with a feather."

She laughed, the sound filled with some of the music that

was Celeste's trademark. "The council members must travel there from time to time. It comes in handy." She frowned. "But it is a weak spot for us. It can just as easily be used to breach the human world."

I thought about her observation. "But that doesn't make sense."

"What doesn't, dear?"

"If there's a door between the worlds, then why would Reginald need to set off an interdimensional breach bomb?"

"Reginald?" Her face leeched a bit more of its color. "You believe he's behind this plot?"

"I do. He's controlling Trudy with poisonous magic. Making her sick. She's little more than a puppet."

She paled, her expression thoughtful. "In answer to your question, the warding only allows creatures from this dimension to come through. Reginald couldn't use it. But this information is concerning. The Dark Fairies have been plotting to overtake the other dimensions for centuries. They are cruel and ruthless leaders. If he's found a way…" She didn't finish the thought. But then she really didn't need to. It was all too clear to me.

Grandmama shoved ineffectually at the covers. "We must tell Katherine."

I stopped her with a hand on her shoulder. "I'll tell her, Grandmama. You rest."

Anger skimmed through her blue-green gaze and faded. She expelled a resigned breath. "Yes. You're right, dear. I need to let the reins go. It's time for the next generation to take over."

"I didn't mean…"

"No. It's true, LA." She reached out and tugged one of my unruly curls, smiling gently. "You'll make a wonderful queen someday."

I flinched, the color leeching from my face. "Oh, I couldn't."

"Yes. You could. And you will. Now if you don't mind. I'm tired. And you need to fill your mother in on things."

I hesitated, waiting as she lay back, her mouth pinched tight as if she were in pain. I was afraid to leave her for fear I'd never talk to her again.

Uncertain what to do, I tugged the covers higher under her chin. Then I gave in to an impulse and bent down, kissing the cool flesh of her cheek.

The skin beneath my lips was etched and thin. I looked down at the array of thin lines covering her once-beautiful face and couldn't believe the change.

My heart twisted painfully.

Something shifted in Celeste's face again. I blinked hard to drive tears away. Finally, I stood with a sad sigh and headed for the door.

A whisper of movement sent an errant red curl dancing against my cheek.

Hesitating, I let the strange feeling wash through me and magically *scented* it. Dark magic. Evil intent.

Panic rising in my chest, I whipped around and saw it.

A man-shaped shadow, ominous in its silence, rising from my Grandmama's sleeping form.

My scream rattled the lamp on Celeste's bedside and brought footsteps thundering down the hall. I didn't wait for help. Flinging my hands up, I etched a trapping spell on the air, a powerful one that Mandy had taught me. The magic shot from my fingertips and hit the wall behind where the wraith had been.

It burned a perfect circle on Celeste's pale yellow wall.

But it didn't even touch the wraith.

The nasty creature was gone.

~

THE DOOR SLAMMED open and Mandy, Brock, Deg and my mother flew in, magic spitting on their fingertips.

I shook my head. "It's gone."

"What's gone?" Mother asked.

"A wraith. It was feeding on Celeste."

Brock and Mandy shared a look.

"What is it?" I demanded, striding over to get in their faces. "What aren't you telling me?"

Brock frowned. "I promise you we didn't know."

"Know what?"

They looked at Mother and Mandy's cheeks flushed. She shoved a ribbon of straight black hair behind her ear. "We were afraid something followed us back from *Axismundi*."

"We saw a shadow...just a brief flicker of movement. But when we looked there was nothing."

Mother hurried over to Celeste and put a hand on grandmama's forehead. A golden light pulsed from her palms and two lines of worry showed up between mother's eyes. "Yes, I sense the residue it left behind." She pulled her hand away and stood staring down at her mother, silvery tears sliding down her cheeks.

I moved over and looped an arm through hers, resting my head on her shoulder. We stood like that, together, for a long moment.

Finally, she moved. "I'll have the room warded."

I nodded. "I'm sorry. I should have caught it sooner."

"It's not your fault, Peaches. Those things are nearly undetectable. Frankly I'm surprised you saw it at all."

I stared down at Grandmama, remembering that she'd wanted me to fill my mother in on the situation with Trudy. I did it quickly, keeping emotion out of it as much as I could and greatly downplaying my time in the catacombs.

Mother had enough to deal with at the moment.

She didn't say anything for a long moment. Finally, she dropped onto the edge of the bed, staring at her hands. "It's been hard losing Trudy. I never believed she meant any real harm. But Celeste is right. We have to err on the side of being too strict. The council cannot be marginalized. The resulting turmoil would create a dangerous world for the humans as well as for us." Rubbing her hands over her slacks, Mother stood up. "I find it hard to believe that Reginald is working alone. He'd need someone with knowledge of our world here. The protections we have in place for just this specific occurrence are nearly impenetrable for a full-scale invading army. He'd need inside help to pull it off. I'm afraid I can't let my sister off the hook on this just yet. But...I'll admit I'm hopeful for the first time in a long while."

She squeezed my hand, giving me a sad smile. "You did well on your mission. I'm sorry I wasn't there to see you off. King Al called an emergency meeting to discuss the breaches." She sighed. "But you found a way in and came back with vital information. I'm proud of you, Peaches."

I shook my head. "I didn't do anything. We don't know anything more now than we did before."

"We do, LA. We know Trudy might be as much a victim of this thing as we are. Or, at the very least, we know that she's not working alone. That's vital information."

"Why?"

"Because I can go to the council and request a limited reprieve for my sister in exchange for her help and information on Reginald." She smiled. "With mother dying..." She blinked several times and then sniffed. "It would be good to have Trudy home. Even under controlled circumstances."

"But the breaches..."

"Reginald has to be a few months away from that yet. The incursions of his monsters into this realm have been infrequent and fairly easily controlled. I know how his twisted mind works. When he's ready to strike he'll distract us with a full-blown attack that will keep us from discovering what he's doing until it's too late."

She seemed pleased by her assessment, but I had to admit it was much less than comforting to me. "You believe Reginald's the one behind all the plots?"

"Not alone, no. He's clearly had some help along the way. Running attacks in twelve separate dimensions is complex and needs many hands. That's why Trudy's input is so vital."

She stared at the burn mark on the wall for a long moment and then stood up. "I need to call the council together. Then once I have her pardon in my hand I can put together a coalition to go and get her."

"Reginald won't just let you take her. He sees Trudy as his ticket to power."

"No. He won't. But if we do it right we'll be in and out of there with my sister before he even knows we've come."

She strode quickly to the door. It was clear from the relaxed and almost happy expression on her face that she was looking forward to the work ahead.

I hated to throw poop on her party cake but…

"What about Grandmama?"

Mother stiffened slightly, one hand on the door.

For the first time I realized my friends had left, probably to give us privacy in our grief.

"I've said my goodbyes. Celeste understands the business of *Familiar, Inc.* and the council must take precedence." She slipped one last, broken glance toward the frail figure on the bed and then fixed me with a gaze tinged in steel. "You'll stay with her until the end. She'll be glad of your presence and I'm sure you'll want to help ease her into *Axismundi.*"

I stared at mother's stiff back moving away from me toward her office, noticing for the first time a new looseness to her usually fitted suit. She'd lost weight over the last weeks. I hadn't even noticed.

I sucked as a daughter.

Deg stepped into the room, giving me a sad smile. "I'm so sorry, LA."

I bit my lip, nodding. "Thanks. Where are the others?"

"I sent them home. I heard your mother tell you to watch over Celeste."

Setting my spine against my doubts, I gave my head a single jerk in the negative. "I can't do that. We have something important we need to do."

He frowned. "More important than saving Celeste?"

"Eminently. She's beyond my help now. But I'm afraid something terrible is about to go down and my mother has no idea what's coming."

"I doubt that, LA…"

"Trust me, Deg. She wasn't there with us. She didn't experience…" Tears burned my eyes as my mind did a flash back of those horrible days in the hole. I clenched my fists against the memory. "Something's not right about all this. Something doesn't make sense. And I'm going to find out what it is."

"How are you going to do that?"

"*We*, Deg. *We're* going to do that. By going back to *Axismundi*."

# CHAPTER FIFTEEN

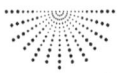

*a* s I prepped for my return to *Axismundi*, I spent a good part of the time kicking myself for not asking my mother the one question that mattered most. I'd gone over and over recent events in my mind, including the events that had brought us to Celeste's current state.

I couldn't shake the idea that they were somehow connected. And that meant I had to take a new look at our previous nemesis. Remembering Celeste's description of the different ways people ended up in the afterlife dimension, I started to wonder about the creature we'd battled weeks earlier.

What part of *Axismundi* had Star been sent to? Had she died when we'd banished her from the warehouse formed in Hell? Or had she simply been banished back to her own world. I was starting to have my doubts that she was well and truly gone.

The front door opened and Deg called out to me.

"I'm in the kitchen." I shoved three small jars filled with shimmering, lively magic into my backpack and added three bottles of water and some protein bars to the contents. If we got stuck in one of the other dimensions for any length of time, I wanted to be ready.

No way was I trusting the food and drink of those alien places again.

Not after seeing what kind of poisonous magic Reginald was capable of wielding.

Deg walked into the kitchen, a big black and green pack slung over one shoulder. "Are you ready?"

"Almost. I just need to feed the cats." I zipped the pack and slipped it over my shoulders. "Come with me. We can leave from the sanctuary."

Deg opened the door into my cat sanctuary and let me walk through first. I glanced his way, noting the taut jaw, brushed with a dark stubble that made him look sexy and dangerous. His dark silver gaze was serious, his lips tipped down in the corners.

He was tense about our incursion back into the afterlife dimension. I didn't blame him. I was worried too. But it was the only way I knew of to discover what was really going on with the barriers.

I filled bowls with food while Deg topped off a giant, communal water bowl. I gave the cats several days' worth, just in case I was gone longer than I expected.

The sanctuary was magicked to look like a small park with a large tree in the center and several smaller trees and bushes positioned around the domed space, their branches stretching over a lush carpet of real grass.

There was a small pond on one end, filled with fish the cats could catch if they desired, and the roof was clear so they could experience the true change of hours throughout the day and night.

There were no birds in my sanctuary. In an enclosed space where cats had the upper hand, that wouldn't have been fair. If my cats wanted to hunt birds, they'd have to leave the sanctuary. A feat they could accomplish with minimal effort by pushing through a small cat door in the back wall.

Deg rejoined me by the back door, dragging his hands over his jeans to dry them.

He gave me an, *Are you sure you want to do this*, look and I smiled.

"Ready?" He jerked his head toward the door. It had a key pad so I quickly punched it in and pulled it open.

"Mandy and Brock were able to get away okay?" I asked.

"They'll meet us in the forest. We'll only have a small window of time to get into the passage. It opens when the moon hits the face of the portal and closes when it moves above it."

I nodded. "That should give us plenty of time. I hope they were able to get the things I asked for."

He shrugged as we stepped out into a cooling night that was moist with a gently falling rain. "Mabel didn't say and I didn't quiz her about it. I'll let you do that."

He lifted dark brows when I threw him a look and I laughed. "Coward."

"Hey, this is your rodeo. I'm not throwing myself onto a bucking bronco unless I absolutely have to."

We started jogging, keeping to the shadows beyond the reproduction style street lights lining my road. The rain pelted us with a gentle relentlessness. The quickly cooling streets gave off the nostril puckering scent of ozone mixed with warm asphalt and exhaust fumes.

I glanced toward the homes on either side of my street as we ran past, noting the warm glow of lights behind some of the windows, and the occasional happy scene of people gathered together around a dinner table, laughing and enjoying each other's company.

I had a sudden nostalgia for the days when my little

family had enjoyed sharing meals together. Those times felt a million miles away as I ran through the wet night, rain dripping down my neck and spinning off into the night in silvery streaks as I shook my head to clear my vision.

Beside me, Deg wasn't even breathing hard. I wondered if he'd used magic as I had to give himself stamina for the trip ahead. Or if it came naturally to him. Judging by the graceful, athletic way he moved, I guessed it was probably the latter.

Since being a clod came natural to me, I let myself enjoy watching him run for a moment. I was pretty sure I looked like a drowned penguin sloughing along behind him through the night.

We reached *Illusory Park* about twenty minutes later and headed directly for the forest. The magical barrier snapped against my skin as we approached, and I saw Mandy and Brock standing just inside the line of energy, under a tree whose dense, overarching branches no doubt kept at least some of the rain off their heads.

Mandy's head snapped up as we approached. "It's about time! We were thinking about going home."

I glanced at the golden orb of the moon hanging in the sky and frowned, realizing for the first time how difficult it was going to be to judge our window. The portal wasn't visible from the forest side, so there was no way to visually judge when it was going to close.

The face of the moon hung behind the dense wall of trees that made up about seventy percent of the primordial forest. And the rocky wall we'd climbed out of when we'd arrived back on the human realm earlier that day didn't really exist from this side.

"How are we going to find this opening?" I asked Brock.

He shrugged. "No clue. But we'd better figure it out quick because that moon is getting pretty high in the sky."

"Freakin' fantastic," I muttered.

The tree behind Brock and Mandy burst into flames, sending chunks of fiery debris flying. Brock and Mandy were flung forward, smashing into Deg and me and sending us all to the ground.

Pain slammed through my shoulder and smoke stung my nostrils. Brock quickly jumped to his feet and, in a flash, morphed into his demonic form and hit the sky.

I would have screamed from the excruciating pain in my shoulder, but Brock had punched me in the stomach when he slammed into me and I was struggling to draw breath.

A delicate hand slapped onto my shoulder, emitting a bright orange glow that squelched the burning ember frying my flesh. Mandy shoved to her feet and started weaving spells on the air as the sound of combat filled the area behind me.

My lungs screeching with every attempt to breathe, I finally managed to pull air into my chest. Nausea filled my mouth with saliva as I pushed to my feet and turned.

The air was dark with demons.

After my first, panicked assessment, I realized there were only a half dozen of the things, but they were enormous and seemed to fill the sky.

I fired energy toward the first flying cockroach and his glowing red eyes focused on me as he easily avoided it. I leaped to the side as the demon lifted its clawed, black hand. The monster's grin was coldly evil as it shot black, focused energy in my direction.

The power arrow hit the ground where I'd been standing, sending dirt and rock six feet into the air.

I fired again and again with similar effects. The things easily avoided my magic.

Above our heads, Brock was doing battle with two of the monsters, barely holding his own. Mandy helped him by distracting the demons with energy arrows, but he still wasn't making any headway that I could see.

*We need to work together,* I told Deg.

*I agree. We need some kind of retaining net. They're avoiding our attacks too easily.*

Mandy's fingers had been dancing on the air, her protective bubble spreading to include us all.

The protection spell shivered violently as it was pelted by successive demonic fire.

Deg looked at her. "With us, Witch."

I reached into my core of shared energy with Deg and, as we'd been practicing, allowed his magic to fuse with mine before drawing it out. His warm, silvery energy reached hungrily for mine, accustomed to the mating that strengthened our individual abilities fourfold and gave us a wider array of powers to work with.

The sphere of silvery energy morphed from a ball into an octopus, its legs sliding into the protrusions of my own energy and closing down, creating an impermeable connection.

With a jolt, I felt a third energy inserting itself into ours and I turned an astonished gaze toward Mandy.

Her smile was slightly embarrassed. She shrugged. "Childhood experiment. It doesn't mean anything."

The heck it didn't. If Deg and I were a matched Witch and Familiar pair, how was another Witch able to insert herself into our shared energy?

That wasn't supposed to be possible.

Deg saw my look and shook his head. "Not the time, LA."

I glared back at him. "Lucy, you have some 'splainin' ta do."

He just shook his head, glancing at Mandy. "On three…"

She nodded. We all lifted our hands.

In my mind, the twirling ball of shimmering silver

energy, turned copper by the insertion of Mandy's power, throbbed expectantly for us to pull it forward.

"Spell?" I asked the Witches.

Mandy gave a jerk of her head, wincing as another demon volley hit the face of her protective bubble. "Take too long." Her voice sounded strained, her words clipped. She was fighting to hold the bubble.

I nodded. "Power word it is then."

Our combined magic began to spin, faster and faster until it broke apart, pieces of it spraying out and cavorting separately in space. A razor thin barrier of energy tied the pieces together and to each of us, but the chunks that had been created with the explosion began to form into letters, dancing and circling on the air until a single word was formed.

All that was left was for the three of us to utter the word. At the exact same time.

I felt Deg and Mandy's concentration and met it with my own.

The magic pulsed in perfect beats, counting down from an internal clock that was mirrored in our brains. As it neared three, I held my breath, giving the magic my full attention.

I felt the moment Mandy's protective bubble slipped away. Its loss left behind a whisper of icy electricity against my skin.

The demons seemed to realize it was gone at the same time. All four of the monsters on the ground turned to us, claws lifted and eyes glowing hotly against terrifying black faces.

Brock screamed in pain and our magic twitched, faltered, and nearly failed as our attention was pulled from the business before us.

But then one of the demons he'd been fighting slammed to the ground in front of the four we'd targeted.

My internal clock shouted, "Go!" And we opened our mouths. *Quiese!*

The word flew away from us like an enormous, copper-colored net, shimmering on the air as it hit the five demons and wrapped tightly around them, tugging them all into a giant wad of monster.

They stood completely still, eyes flashing with mute rage and bodies caught in perfect suspended animation.

While his adversary was distracted by its friends' fate, Brock grabbed him around the throat and, muscles bulging, squeezed until the thing went slack. With a roar, he swung the demon around and released it, sending it toward the tree line where the passage waited.

The air split apart in a silver flash and the demon slipped into the resulting void, disappearing with a giant sucking sound.

Brock dropped wearily to the ground, his enormous wings folding behind him. I looked into his black, still handsome face and smiled. "Nice work. You think you could do the same with this giant magic baggie of boogeys too?"

He looked down at me from his ten foot height and his teeth flashed white in his dark face. "It would be my pleasure."

# CHAPTER SIXTEEN

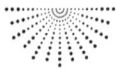

The moon rose close to the treetops as Brock dispatched the bag o' demons into the breach. I noted that the shimmering split in the atmosphere shut with a more determined snap than the first time and realized we were running out of time. If we didn't hurry, the passage would close for the night and we'd lose a day before we could begin our journey.

I took off running, unsure how to reach a passage that appeared to be sitting in the sky, with nothing to climb to get to it except a bunch of smooth-trunked trees.

The trees were hundreds of years old, with trunks whose circumferences measured in yards rather than feet and branches that were easily fifteen feet off the ground.

We weren't climbing those babies.

But the *Illusory Forest*, its roots set in a past that was multi-millennia old, was a trickster beyond understanding. As such, I prayed the way would be shown to us as we got closer.

We'd gone a half mile, the moon hovering just above the treetops, before we stopped, panting and disgruntled.

"We had to have missed it," Mandy grumbled. She glared at me as if I should have known where the stupid thing was. In that moment I forgot, just for a beat, how sad I'd been when I thought she was gone.

Which reminded me. "You never told us how you came to be *here* instead of dead."

"We don't have time for that," Brock said, after skimming Mandy a look filled with meaning.

"Unfortunately, it looks like we have twenty-four hours," Deg told them on a frown.

Brock shook his head. "We need to use the time finding out how to get to this passage or we're going to find ourselves in the exact same spot tomorrow night."

I tilted my head back and stared at the thick wall of trees surrounding us. Though I was unwilling to give up, I realized it clearly wasn't up to me. The magic just didn't seem to be with us at the moment.

Still, something was bothering me. "I wonder..."

"What is it, LA?" Deg asked.

I shook my head, narrowing my gaze on the tree tops. "I don't know. It's just..."

Then it hit me and I had a face-palm moment. "Of course!" Lifting my hands, I crafted a spell on the air, the golden notes of it dancing and swirling around my hands as I created the pieces and then dragged them into coherent forms to shape the magic.

Mandy and Deg watched me carefully, making sounds of recognition as the spell finally rested on the air in front of us. I looked at them and they nodded, finally realizing what I'd figured out.

"What?" Brock asked, completely lost.

"It's the web," I told him. "Everything we do is tied to and controlled by the web." I swung my arm and sent the spell through the air. It exploded before us, the shapes I'd created flaring outward to form what looked like the insides of a computer hard drive. Slowly, the x's and o's formed into a map that highlighted a thousand points of light, each one a distinct shape and color. The size and opacity of each specific point was determined by the magical creature's age and power.

Deg, Mandy and I studied the map carefully, trying to find ourselves on it. After a moment I saw the progressive line of magic surrounding a large, green-tinged area off to one side.

The Park.

"There!" Mandy said, pointing toward four points clustered near the southern park barrier.

I nodded. "Now we need to look for the passage."

"But we have no idea what it looks like," Brock grumbled.

"It's built into the original barrier. Like a small gate." Deg said. "It should be a slightly altered spot on that barrier..." He lifted a finger and pointed to a place where the barrier became less distinct, its edges fuzzy. "Like that."

We all turned toward the spot that corresponded to the gate on the map. There was a large rectangular area in the dirt between two enormous trees where the ground seemed to sparkle. Like a hundred tiny fireflies all resting together on the root-bound soil.

"That's it. Hurry!" Even as I said the words, the rectangle shrunk a few inches and the specks of light dimmed. "It's closing."

I hurried over and stepped into the quickly shrinking space. Immediately, the forest dropped away and I was back inside the rocky passage. The sounds of the forest were a distant chorus, the chirp and scream of nocturnal creatures dulled behind the barrier between *Axismundi* and the human realm.

Mandy and Deg came through right after me and Brock

stepped into the passageway last. The magical blockade snapped closed behind him with a hiss, the sounds of the primordial forest slicing off behind it.

We stood in unnatural darkness for a beat, only the sound of our breathing breaking the stark silence. A ball of yellow light suddenly appeared, casting a sickly hue over Mandy's face. The orb hovered over her palm for a beat and then she lifted her arm and flung it into the passageway ahead of us.

Without a word, Deg and I started off, following the quickly moving light through the twisting passage.

We emerged from the passage a couple of hours later. As before, the area we entered was dark, the earth scorched and filled with dead vegetation. I was starting to wonder if *Axismundi* just gave us what we expected to see, or if it was perpetual midnight there.

It didn't take us long to realize that one thing *had* changed. The horizon was dotted with pulsing blue and orange arcs set equidistantly apart in a semi-circle. The jewel-like skyline encompassed two-thirds of a circle and I had no idea what it meant.

We stopped just outside the opening to the passageway and rested, pulling out bottles of water and energy bars to give us stamina for the next phase of our mission. It would probably be our last chance to rest and eat for a while.

If all went according to plan, things were likely to get squiggy fast. The unpredictable quality of the place would make it necessary for us to stay constantly on our guard.

I had no idea how much time we had before everything exploded around us.

Back in his non-demon form, Brock stood a few feet away from the passage, staring at the pulsing arcs of light in the sky. He'd been uncharacteristically quiet since we'd arrived to find the changes in *Axismundi*. I wondered if he knew the significance and wasn't telling us.

I stood up and went to him, my gaze narrowing in an attempt to see beyond the cloak of darkness smothering the area. "What is it?"

He didn't respond for a long moment. I noted the stiff way he held himself and the clenching of his hands at his sides.

The demon was tense. A fact that increased my own nervousness by a few notches. "Brock?"

He finally glanced down at me, his expression grim. "There's something in the air. I can't describe it. But whatever it is, it has my hackles up. I'm having to fight taking my demonic form."

I frowned. "Describe the emotion. Besides tension. Do you feel fear? Anger?"

"More like expectation. But there's no positive feeling tied to it." He expelled air. "As I said, I can't describe it."

I nodded. Staring off into space, I concentrated on my sensing magic and cast it around us, trying to get a taste of what he was feeling for myself.

I got nothing. "Maybe it's coming from the demonic realm. We *are* close to the barrier, right?"

He nodded. "Very close." He glanced toward Mandy and Deg, his expression softening slightly. "The Witches did good work leading us here."

I nodded. "How long will it take to get to the border?"

"On foot, half a day. But if I fly…"

I shook my head. Though I hated the sound of several hours marching across that forbidding place, I wanted us to stay together. "I'm not comfortable with you going off on your own again."

His handsome face split in a grin that reminded me of his old, cocky self. I realized as my chest tightened at the sight that I'd missed cocky Brock.

Imagine that.

"Aw, you're worried about me? You do care."

I shook my head. "Not in the least. I just don't want to have to explain to the council that I lost their demon."

He chuckled darkly. "That's touching. But I'm afraid you're going to have to trust me on this one." He turned abruptly and headed toward Deg. "Have you located the Nephilim yet?"

Deg looked up from the spell they were weaving on the air. The magic looked like a thousand spiders clambering over each other in the darkness. But, judging by the relaxed expressions on their faces, it appeared to be successful. "We have. She's south of here, just inside the border of the demonic realm. I'm afraid it will take us most of a day to get there."

"On foot, yes. It will only take me a few hours though. I'll go get her and bring her back here. You three deal with Trudy and Reginald."

I opened my mouth to argue but Mandy had already gathered up the spell and collected it into a slightly larger ball of light than the one we'd followed through the passage. She threw it above her head and wiped her hands against her shirt as if they were soiled.

"That will take you to her. But you'll have to find your own way back to this spot." Mandy and Brock shared a look that I couldn't quite read.

"I'm not comfortable with him going alone..." I started to argue.

Deg stood up, shrugging into his pack. "We all have a role to play, LA. Brock's perfectly capable of surviving in this climate. In fact, he's better equipped for it than we are.

"Besides," Mandy said. "None of *us* can fly."

That seemed to be that. I clamped my lips together and accepted that I was outnumbered. "Be careful," I ground out as Brock took off running. Several yards away he leapt off the ground and rose into the black sky, his enormous wings beating the air in a rhythm so powerful I could feel it in my bones.

"Don't look so worried, LA," Deg said softly. He squeezed my shoulder, his touch sending warmth spiraling through me. "He'll be fine."

I nodded, forcing my doubts away. I had bigger problems. Turning to the Witches, I took a deep breath. "I haven't been completely honest with you."

Deg's brows rose. "Oh? About what?"

"I didn't exactly come here to save Trudy from Reginald. Although that's definitely part of my plan."

Mandy frowned, crossing slender arms over her chest. "Then what?"

"I want to find Star."

Silence beat between us for a moment, the air filling with tension.

"And you didn't think that was something we had a right to know?" Mandy finally ground out.

"I did. And I'm sorry. But I was afraid you wouldn't come."

"You'd be right, cat!" Mandy spit back. "That creature nearly killed all of us. Why would you think that here...of all places...we'd come off any better against her?"

"She's dead, LA," Deg interjected. "And she's not connected to this. Why would you want to find her?"

"Are you sure she's dead?" I asked him.

He started to respond and then stopped, expelling air. "No. I guess I can't prove... I just assumed..."

"So did I. But all of this..." I waved a hand to indicate our current situation. "—has made me wonder. What if Star was the first foray into our world? What if she was sent to test how vulnerable we are?"

"You're bat crap crazy, cat!" Mandy growled. "I'm going back." She turned and started toward the passage.

"Two things, Witch…" I said softly. "One, the barrier is closed until morning."

She skidded to a stop, her back ramrod straight. "And two, I'm begging you not to go. I need your help."

My plea hung between us on gossamer strings. I'd never given Mandy the kind of power over me I was offering her. I'd thought I never would. I was the last person who ever wanted to subjugate myself to a Witch.

But desperate times and all that… "Please?"

"Why are you so sure she's part of this?" Deg asked.

I shrugged. "I just am. I can't explain it. Can't you trust me?" I asked him.

He held my gaze, his attractive silver eyes filled with questions. But to his credit, he didn't ask them. Deg nodded. "Of course I trust you."

His trust met an answering emotion in me. Something that felt like the beginnings of tenderness rose up, making it hard to breathe.

"Tell us what you have in mind," he urged.

I looked at Mandy and she slowly turned, her expression angry. But the anger didn't fill her gaze. There was curiosity there. She inclined her head and I breathed deeply for the first time in moments. "I need to tap into my tracking magics and I'll probably need your help." I told her. I glanced at Deg. "Mandy and I connected with her that one time, a direct magic channel."

Mandy nodded. "Yes. And I was nearly killed, but the kitten intervened." Her eyes widened. "Ah…that's what you want with the Nephilim."

"Yes. I've been thinking about it and I realized that Mabel has the ability to neuter dark energy. She's like a buffer between us and evil magic. If we can draw Star here…"

Deg threw up a hand. "Wait...you want to bring her to us?"

"I think that's best, don't you? We're on relatively well-known ground here. We're close to Trudy and the demonic realm. And the Heavenly realm is near enough to reach in a few hours."

Something like respect danced through Mandy's expression. "You've thought this all out haven't you?"

I nodded.

"And Trudy?"

That part of my plan was the murkiest. It was complicated by the imminent arrival of the council, led by my mother.

She was going to kill me. But, at least I was in the right place if she did.

"I'm hoping we can draw Reginald away from Trudy and Mother and the council can protect her. But if worse comes to worse..."

"You'll whisk her into the Heavenly realm," Deg finished for me.

"Yes."

He thought about it for a moment. "Okay, say we manage to draw Star to us. What then? Are we going to bitch-slap her into telling us who's behind the breaches?"

"That didn't work out so well for us last time," Mandy mumbled.

"If I'm right, she had some help from *Axismundi* the last time," I told them. "Hopefully that won't be the case here and now."

"You think Reginald was feeding her power?"

"Somebody was," I frowned. "It could have been him."

"I don't understand, cat. Are we back to thinking dear old Auntie is evil?"

I really wasn't. But since I had no idea who *was* behind

the current problem, I hesitated to rule Trudy out. "That's what we're here to find out."

"The Nephilim seems to trust your aunt." Deg reminded me.

"How do we know we can trust *her*?" Mandy arched an inquisitive brow. "Yeah, it seems like she's been helping us, but what if she's just been leading us down a path?"

I had to admit the question was a valid one. "Okay, you're right. I shouldn't trust Mabel just because my perception is that she's on our side. The truth is, we really don't have any idea who's on our side right now."

"We're going to proceed assuming everybody's out to get us?" Deg asked, frowning. "That's a much better strategy."

"Sorry?" I offered in an apologetic tone.

"No, you're right. But I don't have to like it." He gave me a crooked grin that made my heart go pitty-pat.

I smiled back. "Which brings us back to Star. At least, we know for sure we can't trust *her*."

"I'll cling to that with both hands," groused Mandy. "So, let's find that evil critter. Brock's going to be back with the Nephilim soon."

I nodded, pulling off my pack. "I brought some things we'll need."

Mandy slipped a hand into her back pack. "I have my tracking magics. I made some that are keyed to finding demonic entities..." She looked up to find Deg and I staring. The Witch shrugged. "What? I didn't like losing the big lug before. If we lose him again I want to be prepared."

Deg tugged his pack off his back. "I brought something too." He reached inside and pulled out a folded square of fabric. Shaking it out with a snap of his wrists, he carefully spread it on the ground.

I clapped my hands in delight. "It's like my rug!" The large square of black fabric had a protective circle painted on it, the paint infused with Rosemary. "I smell lavender and coconut. But there's something else…"

"Myrrh," Deg told us.

"Ancient protective herb," Mandy said, nodding in approval. "You added the oils to the paint, I assume?"

"Yes. The fabric is woven of thin bamboo fibers for additional protection and banishment of evil." He pointed to the four small bags sewn to the corners. "Those hex bags contain rosemary, thyme, salt and cumin."

"I love this," I told him. "Pure genius. The only bad thing about my rug is it's not really portable."

He smiled. "I made one for all of us. It's a handy thing to have around."

"Clearly," Mandy said in her snotty voice. "Since we're already using it." She was glaring at the fabric but her eyes were sparkling. She loved it. But she wouldn't tell Deg that to save her life.

Pulling two of my three jars out of the pack, I set them on the cloth. "Exorcism spell. I've altered it to pull dark energy from a demonic force and weaken it."

"What's the other one?" Deg asked.

"A special tracking spell. If she does manage to get away, this will make it easy to follow her."

Mandy placed a thick, white candle in the center of the cloth, settling a crescent-shaped, blade next to it. The ceremonial knife had a white bone handle, carved with spells to enhance magic. She dug around in the pack again until she came up with a small jar filled with silvery green magic. "At least now I know why you asked me to bring this."

The stalking spell was identical to the one we'd used the last time we'd tracked Star. The blade was something new. If we were going to use the spell to track the demon a second time, we'd need a drop of blood that would recall the spell to our previous attempt.

Mandy placed the spell jar at the center of our protective circle and opened it. The magic inside began to swirl with expectation. The Witch looked at me and then at Deg.

We all stepped inside the circle at the same time. Deg lifted his hands and danced his fingers on the air, speaking the magic to close the circle. A beat later it snapped shut with a sizzle. Mandy reached for the Boline.

She quickly sliced the curved blade over the tip of her index finger and squeezed a drop of blood into the potion. It surged up in a froth that reached the top of the jar and hung there, just at the edge of the glass. Mandy spoke the Latin word for *seek*. "*Quaerere.*"

I extended my hand and she made a short slice across my palm. I said the word *follow* in Latin. "*Sequitur,*" as I allowed a drop of my blood to fall into the spell. The potion bubbled up, oozing thickly over the lip of the jar. It didn't dribble down the sides, but rather clung to the atmosphere above the jar, boiling as if over a flame.

Deg placed his hand over ours and Mandy made a slightly longer slice across the back of his hand. He opened his mouth and spoke, "*inveniet!*" which meant *find* in Latin.

Our hands still joined, we moved them over the potion and allowed Deg's blood to join ours in the jar. A bubble shot up and popped around the drops of blood and the roiling mix burst into the air, the particles turning to mist as we began chanting the spell. The green-tinged mist rose above our heads, more vibrant and aggressive with the addition of Deg's magic and our blood. It spun so rapidly I started to be afraid that it might spin away, escaping the protective spell and evading our control.

But Deg's circle held. The mist rose up to fill it, creating a circular column of silvery green that rose several feet above our heads.

Magic filled the circle, its sulfurous scent making my

nose twitch and calling to my own energy, which throbbed against my skin in time to my rising heartbeats. Mandy's fingers were cool in mine, her grip loose. Deg's touch was hot and dry.

The feel of the tracking magic was as recognizable as it was different. Deg's protections were a buffer that made the swirling magic slow and calm, the combined scent of the herbs he'd used in the cloth filling the air to ease the stinging sulfur stench.

Within its embrace the elemental building blocks of stalking energy formed a passage through the layers of time and space.

If it worked the way we'd planned, the magic would create a portal that allowed us to visualize Star's location. Then it would be up to me to immobilize her before she got the upper hand.

A swirling black hole opened in the air beyond the circle's influence.

There was no sign of Star. But I knew from before that she could be hidden behind a curtain of obscuring magics.

I felt her presence within the portal.

Fortunately, there was no painful warding like the last time when we located her. Only a thick resistance, like steel fibers trying to block out our stalking energy.

Slowly, the mist lightened, turning charcoal gray, and I could see the outline of a slender face through its opaque surface. We chanted faster, our words merging so completely I couldn't tell one voice from the other. Our voices rose, spinning louder and faster as the magic spilled from our throats and danced within the mist surrounding us.

The magical energy lightened another shade. Until I could make out the thick fall of golden hair and, finally, a pair of wide blue eyes filled with murderous hate.

*Star!*

The blue gaze widened. The finely shaped brows rose. Our quarry recognized the magic and knew that we'd found her.

Excitement pulsed in my throat. I risked a glance down toward the immobilizing spell. I would need to grab it soon...

The magic shifted, wobbled, and the portal started to shrink.

We were going to lose her.

Our voices rose in the night, lifted higher, and sank more deeply into the fabric of the atmosphere, throbbing in my head.

The portal stopped shrinking, began to grow again, and the hate in those blue eyes deepened. The last of the haze within the portal disappeared with a hiss and I saw her face.

Beautiful and cold like polished marble. I realized she'd been hiding her true beauty behind a mask when she was in the human realm, creating a persona that no one would notice. Just another drone moving through the motions at *Familiar, Inc.*

She'd played us like a Witch's fiddle. With a master's practiced touch.

I grudgingly accepted her dominance, even as I swore it would never happen again.

Then she smiled.

And in the next moment I knew things weren't going to go as planned.

The silvery green mist inside the circle began to spin with agitation. The stalking magic sped and sped until it became an impossible force that swelled and battered against the restraints we'd given it.

With nowhere else to go, the energy turned on us, pounding against my skin until all I knew was pain and the hypnotic swirl of silver-green light.

Our warding wasn't up to the attack.

The circle gave way with a sound like fire grabbing oxygen just before it exploded, and we were all blown away from the circle.

I sailed through the air, flailing and helpless against the crushing momentum.

I hit a spiky tree with a bone shattering crunch. Bright misery swept through me in a wash. I slid down the prickly trunk and hit the ground hard enough to crack the bones in my lower back.

I lay there whimpering, pain turning me limp on the blackened ground.

Despite my dire condition, a sense of imminent danger brought my head up and made my eyes widen. Someone stood in the center of the protective circle.

She was tall and slim, with fingers that were like claws and legs set wide in a battle stance. Her eyes glowed a deadly blue, energy boiling behind them.

I recognized her hated face behind the haze.

*Star*.

Knowing it meant my life, I tried to shove off the ground. But I was as weak as a kitten and my arms gave out beneath me. When I tried to move again I realized that one arm was completely numb.

My gaze scanned the ground looking for the immobilizing spell. I couldn't see it. My heart pounded as panic swelled. The thing I'd counted on to stop Star was gone.

I spared a moment to wonder if Deg and Mandy were okay. I prayed they were. A horrible sense of déjà vu slid through me. *Axismundi* was back to ripping my friends away.

I tried to push to my feet again, finally managing to climb to my knees. Agony radiated through my shoulder and I looked down, finding a spike as long as my forearm speared clean through my flesh.

I wobbled, dizziness swamping me, and thought I might pass out.

Instead, something worse was waiting for me.

Star lifted a hand. As if savoring the moment, she slowly squeezed it closed, her lips curving upward.

A horrific pressure filled my chest.

She closed her fingers a little more, her smile widening.

I fought to stay upright but my chest felt like it was buried under a pile of boulders.

My heartbeat slowed beneath the pressure and my head pounded. The feeling of compression was so horrific my screams were locked behind it, unable to escape my gasping lips.

Star's hand tightened more and the agony in my chest deepened. She was literally crushing my heart.

I gasped out a cry. Desperation giving me strength, I shoved to my feet and stumbled toward her. I tried to wrap my mind around a magic word to stop her but I couldn't think through the pain.

She watched me come, the smile never wavering.

My feet felt like lead. As if they belonged to someone else. I took a step and something gave. My ankle twisted and I slammed to the ground mere feet away from Star.

Her laughter was like razors against my ears.

Thoughts skittered away. My limbs turned nerveless and I realized I wasn't getting up again.

Star moved closer, bending to look down at me. Her hated face filled with malicious pleasure. "We meet again, Familiar."

I opened my mouth to curse her.

And the world exploded in a sea of golden light.

## CHAPTER SEVENTEEN

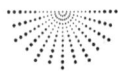

$\mathcal{T}$he light burned my eyes and I had to close them. Heat slammed into me under the searing radiance. For a moment I thought I was on fire. The pain was a living thing, digging into my chest and flowing through my bones like liquid flame.

Fortunately, it quickly started to recede and, when the last of it had eased away, my heart no longer felt as if an invisible hand was squeezing it. I shoved to my feet, realizing that my bones didn't hurt anymore either.

My shoulder was healed.

I looked around, finding Deg and Mandy and reassuring myself that they were okay. Then I sought out the source of the light. Because once I'd figured out what was happening, I knew who had to be behind it.

Mabel.

She was standing next to Star, one hand resting on the other creature's arm and her gaze focused on Star's too-pretty face.

Star was still as stone. Only her hate-filled eyes moved.

"What did you do to her?" I asked the Nephilim.

Mabel turned to me with a frown. "You shouldn't have come back."

I stopped a few feet away, surveying the wreckage of Deg's beautiful protective cloth and the broken and spilled contents of my spell jars.

So much for planning ahead.

"I had to. Something's not right."

Mabel shook her head with child-like irritation. I could almost picture her stamping a foot. But, despite her size and appearance, the Nephilim had been alive several times longer than I had. "Of course it's not right, LA. The worlds are converging. They're on a path of self-destruction. The only hope for you now is for each dimension to buckle down and find a way to protect themselves when the end comes."

I blinked, turning to Deg as he joined me. Mandy came up on my other side, a silent ally.

"Well, that's a different tune from the one you were singing earlier," I told her.

Mabel shrugged. "I tried to stop this. But I haven't been successful. Now we need to prepare for the worst."

"Don't give up so easily," Deg told her. "We have a plan."

Mabel's golden brows rose. "Do you? Does it include this?" She lifted her free hand to indicate Star.

"Yes," I agreed. "But it involves you too. Don't give up on us, Mabel."

The Nephilim expelled air in a long, heartfelt sigh. The perfect skin between her brows furrowed prettily. "Reginald has gone underground. No one can find him. The breaches have already begun in nine of the dimensions."

"Which ones are still intact?" Deg asked.

"Demonic, Heavenly and human."

Understanding lit. "That's why Brock isn't with you."

She nodded. "He left me after I promised I'd come to you.

He can do no good there. The breaches are going off in a clockwise order. The demonic realm is next."

"Then us," Mandy mumbled, her gaze sliding to the passage we'd used to enter *Axismundi*.

"Yes. I can help you get back through the gate," Mabel said. "Go home and try to hold out against the attack. Maybe you'll get lucky."

"No!" I walked over and stood close, feeling the hate beaming from Star's gaze as it fixed on me. "Mabel, we can fight this."

"You cannot."

"Why? How are the breaches happening? Surely there are protections…"

"Of course!" She frowned, unhappy with me. "But there is a key. Whoever has the key is using it to get past the barriers."

"What key?" I asked.

But Deg had already figured it out. "Heaven."

The Nephilim nodded. "A precise set of notes from the heavenly choir. Thought to be safe because of its inaccessibility to all but a rare few. Its unattainable nature was all the protection it needed."

"But Reginald somehow got the key," I breathed. The worst had happened.

A distant boom shook the ground beneath our feet. I grabbed for Deg to keep from going down.

Mabel and Star were untouched by the explosion.

The distant horizon turned orange and blue, creating a perfect arc in the sky that matched the others.

The demonic realm had fallen.

"We're out of time. I need to question her."

Mabel eyed me for a long moment and then nodded. She stepped away from Star, a golden thread trailing from each of her small fingers.

Mabel had a magic leash on the demon.

As she stepped back, Star seemed to shiver. Her chest rose and fell once, and her hateful gaze slid to me. "You haven't learned your lesson, I see."

"Tell us who's behind all this."

She laughed, the sound surprisingly rough in her delicate throat. "Nice try, rodent."

"Show some respect, you evil shrew," Mandy said. She reached out and touched Star on the arm and jagged blue-black bolts of electricity burned over the demon's skin, leaving scorch marks behind where they touched.

Star's teeth clacked together and her eyes rolled back in her head, but when the energy stopped, she drew herself up and licked her lips. "Thank you for that, Witch."

Mandy smiled too. "You're welcome. There's more where that came from."

"I know you've been working with him, Star. Tell us where Reginald is. Whatever he's promised you, he's not going to pay up. Once his plan is initiated he'll forget you exist."

Star stared at me for a moment and then cocked her head. A shiny ribbon of golden hair dropped to one slender shoulder. She looked too much like an Angel for my comfort.

I preferred my evil nemesis to come with warts and stringy, grease-laden hair so she was easily identified.

"Reginald?" She frowned prettily. "Fascinating."

Mandy snapped her fingers and rings of spitting electricity encircled the creature, the volts searing her pale skin and sending the reek of burning hair into the air.

I grimaced as it went on for a minute longer than before.

Star looked decidedly less chipper about it the second time. Which made me happy. "Just tell us where he is, Star."

She skimmed a hostile glance to Mandy, thoughtfully

pursing her lips. As another minute crept by, Mandy lifted her hand, fingers pressed together to snap.

Star shook her head. "That won't be necessary, Witch. It's no skin off my nose if you take Reginald. In fact, that would help immensely. Have at him. But I don't envy you the job." She gave Deg and me an evil smile. "I wish I could come with. I'm sure you'll enjoy returning to the catacombs. I know you have a fondness for the place."

My PULSE PICKED up another notch with every step we took closer to the hated prison. Blood thundered through my veins like a herd of charging bulls. Sweat trickled down between my shoulder blades, soaking my shirt, and my breath whistled out from my lungs, the wheezing sound so loud in the passageway I was certain one of the prison guards could follow the sound to find us.

Mabel stepped up beside me, throwing me a worried glance. She'd replaced her shimmery robes with a really cool getup of leather and denim. "Are you certain you'll be okay?" she asked.

I squinted at her in the low light. Maybe it was just the grown-up outfit, but she looked to me like she'd added a few human years since beginning our journey together. "I'm fine. Why does everybody keep asking me that?"

"Because I've seen ghosts with more color in their faces," Mandy whispered.

"And drier people stepping from a swimming pool," Deg added.

The Nephilim nodded. "I could close my eyes and follow the sound of your breathing alone. I believe I've encountered such breathing before…observing a water buffalo in Asia."

"Okay, okay. I get it. Yeah, I'm about to pee my pants. But

you haven't been here before. You don't understand how bad this place is."

Deg lifted his brows.

"Except for Deg. He understands."

"I *do* understand. But we have help now, LA. It will be fine." Despite his brave words, I noticed a sheen on his upper lip and the way his head kept swiveling in search of guards.

"Whatever." I looked at Mabel. "How are we going to find Reginald?"

"I'll find him. He leaves a very strong magic signature behind. It stains his aura from the dark magic he's used. He'll be like a lamp in the darkness of those caves."

"I can't believe a guy like ol' Reggie would lower himself to hide down here." I shook my head.

"Don't let the tidy royal act fool you, LA. He got his stripes in the streets of *Axismundi*. He's a tough scrapper and he's just about as savvy as they come."

I nodded, not doubting a word of it. "I wonder if mother and the council have arrived at Trudy's yet. It should be about time."

Mabel frowned. "I hope their travels were successful. Things are not as they usually are in *Mundala*."

Worry spiked through me. "Oh great! Thanks for that. As if I didn't already have enough to worry about."

The Nephilim simply shrugged.

We rounded a bend in the passage and Mabel put out an arm, stopping us. She listened carefully, looking around before nodding her head for us to move forward. She ushered Mandy and Deg past and then fell in with me.

I peered into the darkness, seeing the subtle glow of the long row of holes in the floor. My skin went clammy and nausea bloomed in my gut at the memory of that horrible cell. My feet got caught up in each other and it was all I could do to keep from falling to the floor.

Mabel grasped my arm. "Stay strong, LA. All will be well. I promise. I'm very sorry you must do this."

"Let me out, you death-world pigs!" an enraged voice shouted

My companions skidded to a halt. I nearly bumped into them before I could stop too.

Mandy started forward, her expression filled with rage. Deg just barely managed to grab her arm. "Slow down, Witch!"

"He's here, Deg! What kind of treachery is this?"

"Was that…?"

I didn't get a chance to finish. The shadows around us shifted and several prison guards bled into the light, their massive forms every bit as terrifying as I remembered.

Two of them swung muscle-bound arms, their fists smashing into Deg and Mandy and sending them to the ground. I lifted my arms, intending to hit them with whatever magic I could muster.

A soft hand grabbed my wrist and I heard a click.

My horrified gaze fell to my wrist and then rose to the pretty face of the Nephilim. A silvery track of tears slipped down her flawless face. "I'm so sorry, LA."

My head started to shake before the full meaning of her apology sank in. "No…"

Mabel turned away and started walking. Two of the guards scooped up my friends and followed her. The rest of the guards parted, their heads dropping to their chests as another soldier, taller and much more good-looking than the rest, strode through the ranks and stopped in front of me.

He smiled. "Hello again, Ms. Mapes."

*Trudy's handsome soldier!*

Big hands grabbed for my arms and I jerked away. "What is this about? Let me go! And release my friends, immediately!"

He stared at me a moment, his smile softening. "From the moment I laid eyes on you I knew. You bear the same familial marks. The same proud carriage. The same slightly arrogant tilt of the chin. You remind me so much of her. But stronger…" He reached out and touched my jaw with a strangely gentle finger.

I tried to bite his hand.

He jerked away and nodded appreciatively. "Spunkier too. Trudy would have been fine if she'd had even half your spunk." He jerked his head toward his men and turned away, striding back in the direction he'd come.

I was grabbed up and dragged in his trail, screaming and trying to kick and bite the guards who were holding me. I'd kill them all before I let them take me back to that cell.

It didn't take me long to figure out I needn't worry.

Not about going back to the cell at least.

But there was still plenty of stuff to worry about.

# CHAPTER EIGHTEEN

*I* was dragged to the room where I'd first laid eyes on Trudy and flung down onto the grass in front of her empty throne. The enormous room was empty, the castle too quiet.

I wondered again if the council had managed to extricate Trudy.

The door leading to Trudy's rooms opened and closed, and footsteps sounded on the hard stone path.

I shoved hair out of my face and pushed to my feet, scrubbing a hand over my cheeks to dry the angry tears there. My stomach twisted painfully at Mabel's betrayal and worry for my friends made my chest tight.

I had to convince Trudy to help me get out of there. My friends needed me to spring them from those horrible cells.

But it wasn't my aunt who strode quickly toward me. I glared at Reginald, his cold, handsome face a mask of unconcern. "Ms. Mapes. It's good to see you again."

"Go to Hell."

His smile was cool and he nodded, stopping far enough

away from me that I couldn't launch myself at him and claw out his eyes.

Smart move.

"I know you're angry…"

"Angry?" I barked out a laugh. "I passed that several exits ago. I'm spitting mad. And if you'll step a little closer I'd be glad to demonstrate." My cat energy bubbled below my skin, but a quick shock of pain along my nerve endings reminded me I was cuffed so I forced it back.

Reggie leaned against the arm of the big throne. "I don't think I'd like that, LA. I can call you LA, can't I? Or would you prefer LeeAnn?"

"I'd prefer that you come over here so I can rip a few pieces off your smug hide."

"We can use that anger." He slid into the throne, sitting forward and resting his arms on his elegantly clad knees. "I need your help."

I was stunned to momentary silence. The gall of the man… I sputtered my outrage for a beat and then forced myself to calm so I could speak. "You need *my* help? Good luck with that."

"Actually, I think you're going to find that it's in your best interests to work with me."

"Oh, *do* you think that? Delusion isn't a good look on you, *Reggie*." I spat his name with emphasis, intending to annoy him.

If he was annoyed he hid it well. He simply nodded. "It's absolutely true. If you want to save your aunt…"

"Don't you dare threaten her again! I hope she's safe with my mother. You've hurt her enough."

He stared at me a long moment. Then he looked down at his hands. Something within him shifted, softened. I realized he was about to go into *cajole and convince* mode. I wasn't going to let it happen.

"Don't bother trying to sweet talk me. I'm not stupid enough to fall for your lies."

*I hoped I wasn't that stupid anyway. But I was feeling pretty desperate.*

Anger finally filtered through his gaze. "You have no idea what's going on here, Familiar. You've been coddled and spoiled all your life. You've been protected from the less savory aspects of your family." He stood up and moved close, one hand outstretched and the fingers misted with angry looking charcoal gray energy.

I felt the sting of his energy just before my muscles seized up. I couldn't move...could barely breath past the power he was using to immobilize me.

Reggie leaned close, his hot breath bathing my face. "Trudy is the monster here. Not I."

I blinked under the explosion of his words against my skin. I wanted to shake my head, to argue, but I saw in his gaze that he meant every word. He was telling me the truth as he knew it.

Our eyes held, mine filled with hatred and his dark with rage. Neither one of us was going to give.

After a moment he sighed and dropped his hand. Movement immediately returned to my limbs. "Look, LA, I know you want to believe the best of your aunt. But you have to be wondering why she was banished here in the first place."

"I know why. She tried to undermine the council."

His upper lip curled. "That's a very mild way of putting it. Trudy tried to have several members of the council killed." When I gasped, his expression softened. "The only reason she wasn't put to death was her relationship to your mother and grandmother. Her banishment was meant to end the danger. I only wish it had worked."

"If that's true...and I'm not saying it is...how did she manage to rise to queen?"

"She isn't queen, LA. She's only a figurehead. One that I've presented to the creatures who live here because it suited both of us. Trudy got her power and status, I had a means to an end..."

"What end?"

He frowned. "Equality among all the magic houses. I've lived what it's like to be considered lesser, LA. Trust me, you don't want to experience what I grew up with. Dark Fairies are hated, distrusted, merely because of the source of our magic."

"Death magic versus life magic," I sneered. "Yeah, I can see why you'd have trouble deciding which is better." I shook my head as he bristled.

"Dark energy is just a different type of magic. Why should some random entity be able to decide that white energy is better? Why should the Witches and the Familiars be at the top of the food chain? Why should the Angels be considered above the rest of us? True happiness throughout the dimensions won't be achieved until we're all equal. That is my dream. And through your aunt I nearly gained it."

"Nearly?" I asked, hoping he would tell me what I wanted to hear. That Trudy had escaped with my mother to the human dimension.

"Yes, unfortunately, my figurehead was...is...much too ambitious to allow me to hold her back for long. With unwitting help, she's thrown off my magic and escaped. I believe at this very moment she's on her way to the Heavenly realm. She means to breech the gates." He stepped closer, lowering his head and fixing me with a dark gaze filled with deadly intensity. "She means to pull all twelve dimensions under her control."

I shook my head. "She can't get into Heaven. The gates are immune to Familiar magic."

"Ah, but there's one type of magic they aren't immune to."

Mabel's words came back to me. *The Dark Faeries have never tried to breach the Heavenly barrier.* "Dark Fairy magic? But she doesn't have that, does she?"

"No. She has something better. She has Nephilim energy. They're like a walking, talking key to the Heavenly realm."

I frowned. "Mabel? She'd never..."

"Not your pretty young friend, LA. Have you not wondered why you haven't clapped eyes on her brothers since coming here?"

My breath caught in my throat. My stomach twisted. Suddenly Mabel's recent treachery made perfect sense. "Trudy has them?"

"Yes. And as long as she does, all twelve dimensions are in grave and imminent danger."

"If that's true, then you need Mabel. She should be able to help her brothers."

"She would if she could. But Trudy has turned Mack and Ralph against her. They won't listen to their sister's wise council." He smiled grimly. "No, LA. Like it or not, I'm afraid you and I are stuck with each other. You see, as things stand now, you're the only one who can stop your aunt."

"What do you mean?" I asked him before I thought better of it.

He shrugged. "I have no leverage over her. Trudy cares about very few things. One of those things is family."

My laugh was harsh. "You mean the family that banished her here? She isn't going to care what I think. I barely know her."

"You're mistaken, LeeAnn. She does care. Very much."

I should have known I was in trouble when his gaze went shrewd. Unfortunately, I was distracted by the idea of Trudy caring about what happened to me.

*Was it possible?*

Rough hands grasped my arms before I could react. My

legs were knocked out from under me and I fell to the grass. I realized for the first time that there was something in the grass. A silvery kind of netting which I quickly found wrapped around me. The mesh tightened as soon as it touched my skin and compressed against me until I panicked.

Struggling did no good at all. The mesh only tightened until it cut into my bare flesh.

I screamed, part rage and part pure, animal fear. A shadow fell over me and I looked up into Reggie's hated gaze. He looked appropriately somber. "I really am sorry about this, LeeAnn. I'd hoped you'd help us willingly. But since you're determined to defy me..." He let the thought trail away, his implication clear.

If I wasn't going to help him capture my aunt willingly. He'd force me to help him trap her.

I barely noticed when the guards hefted me off the ground and dropped me on a wagon. All I could think of was my friends, deep in the bowels of hell in the catacombs.

And there was nobody left who could help them.

# CHAPTER NINETEEN

*I*'m not sure when I became aware that we were going the wrong way. I think it might have been when we set upon the demon pathway I remembered all too well.

We weren't heading to the Heavenly dimension.

We were heading toward home.

Panic clawed through me, making my heart race. If we were heading toward the human dimension that meant Trudy was there.

Along with my mother, our friends and allies.

And possibly Celeste.

I couldn't just lie there while they were in danger.

I forced myself to calm, controlling my breathing and slowing my heartrate until I could think again. I had to get out of that webbing.

I tested it with a small infusion of magic and pain radiated through my wrist.

I'd forgotten about the cuff. But it hadn't stopped me before. It had merely slowed me down a little. If I could just shift into my cat…

"How are you, LeeAnn? Comfy?" Reggie asked.

I didn't bother answering him. He knew darn well I was miserable. And seriously peeved. Plus, I felt like a sausage wearing ugly jewelry.

"I'm sure you'll be glad to be home. I know your mother will be happy to see you."

The very purposeful way he'd mentioned my mother told me all I needed to know about his plans. He wasn't going to use me to entice Trudy at all. Or at least not only her.

He was going to use me against my mother.

I frowned. What possible purpose would that serve him?

Unless he couldn't break through the human realm as he had the others...

Then it hit me. The obvious answer.

"Sir?"

Reggie glanced up as the handsome guard I'd thought was Trudy's friend addressed him. The man bowed slightly and skimmed me a look as he straightened. "We've sensed foreign magic near the bogs."

Reggie glared at the guard. "Well, then take care of it. Do I have to do everything?"

The night behind Reggie and the guard exploded. The guard's hand snaked out and Reggie was suddenly flying through the air. Wasting no time, the guard bent over the wagon. I tried to shrink away but couldn't move.

Frowning as chaos exploded around us, the guard ran a strange looking object over the mesh and it fell away.

More explosions and shouting increased the activity in the ranks of Reggie's soldiers. They were running everywhere, weapons drawn. Some of them shed their armor and took to the sky.

Trudy's guard offered me a hand and, after a moment's hesitation, I accepted it. He helped me out of the wagon, fixing me with a stern look. "Can you shift?"

I rubbed the torn skin where the mesh had been. "I think so."

"Do it then and get out of sight." He turned and ran into the fray before I could ask him what was going on.

A white-hot bolt of pure energy sheared past, ripping the planks of the wagon I'd recently inhabited into kindling.

I ducked behind what was left and spotted Reggie on the ground. His eyes were open and he was lying very still, but I could tell by the rise and fall of his chest that he was still alive. I had no idea what the soldier had done to him. Judging by the enraged glint in his eyes the man would pay dearly if he was captured.

I forced my gaze away from the evil wizard and grabbed for my shifting magic, visualizing my cat even as I braced for the bracelets to fight back. The result was as violent as I'd expected. The explosion of energy blew the wagon away from me. Reggie's stiff form whooshed away with it, smacking hard against the remaining tatters of lumber and sliding to the ground in a heap.

I really hoped that hurt.

Agony ripped up my arm and speared my chest as my body arched, twisted, and formed claws and fur. I gritted my teeth and leapt into the air to aid the change.

I landed hard, my feline limbs only half formed, and screamed as pain ratcheted through me from the cuff. The sound came out as a feline yowl.

The cuff was white hot against my flesh, the stench of burning fur mixing with the sulfurous leavings of exploding magic. In sheer desperation I shook the leg still inside the cuff and it scraped free.

The pain immediately disappeared. I lay there panting for a beat. Until another energy bolt tore the ground up a foot away from me.

I leapt up and ran into the underbrush, intending to circle around and help whoever was firing at Reggie's soldiers.

The scent of another cat teased my nostrils as I took off running. I screeched to a halt when the animal stepped out from behind a tree. I hissed as I recognized Mack, Mabel's brother. *If you're here to try to stop me, don't count on it.* I told him. *I'm done being shoved around and abused.*

*I don't want to stop you. Mabel sent me to get you. Things have gotten complicated in the human realm. Your mother needs you.*

I thought about what he was saying for a moment, trying to piece together something that felt real. I'd been told so many conflicting stories since the current adventure started that I had no idea whom or what to trust. *I was told you were working for Trudy against the human realm. Why should I trust you?*

Even as I asked him the question, I knew that story was probably false. Reggie hadn't taken me to the heavenly realm because that wasn't where Trudy was, apparently.

I felt the kitten frown in my mind. *Haven't we proven our loyalty to you again and again?*

*Your sister has. Until she betrayed me to Reginald.*

He shook his head, sneezing. He sat down, licking a paw and wiping it over his nose as his voice filled my mind. *That couldn't be helped. Reginald was starting to distrust Mabel. She needed to prove her loyalty. But we knew he wouldn't hurt you. He plans to trade you for your mother's spot on the council. And we intended to rescue you anyway.*

*Very handy excuse.* I turned back the way we'd come. Back toward the catacombs.

*Where are you going? I wasn't lying, LA. We need to go back.*

*I have to save my friends. Then I'll happily go back home and let all you jerks clean up your own mess.*

*Your friends are here. Who do you think is fighting Reginald?*

Hope soared. *All of them?*

*Yes. They're fighting alongside my sister.*

I reached out for Deg, tentatively prying open our private communication channel. *Deg?*

There was a bit of static and then nothing. *You're lying.*

*I'm not. He's probably just busy...*

*LA?*

Relief spun through me. I dropped to my haunches as my limbs went weak with it. *Are you all right?*

*Yes. Are you?*

*I'm alive. I was just coming to look for you guys. Brock and Mandy are all right too?*

*Yes. And you can't stay here, LA. You need to go home. We'll be right behind you. Go with Mack.*

I hesitated a beat and then realized what he was telling me. My mother and our friends were in danger as I'd suspected. Mack had been telling me the truth. *I'm not leaving you. I'll help here and then we'll all go home.*

*No. Time is short. And LA, there's something else you need to know.*

I'd stopped listening, my mind was occupied with trying to come up with an argument for staying with my friends. But the urgency in his voice captured my straying attention. *What's wrong?*

*The demonic realm is still intact. It hasn't been breached.*

I thought about the surprising news for a beat, a dozen questions rising in my mind. *But we saw it fall.*

*No. We saw what someone wanted us to see. Brock was there. He said it was still intact when he was captured. And that the guards at the prison were bragging about the demons being stronger than all the others.*

*But why...?*

*I don't know. But it's important somehow. The answer is at home. And we need you to find it.*

I gave up fighting the inevitable. He was right. I needed to go back. *Stay safe, okay. I'll see you at home.*

*Take care, LA. Someone we know is behind all this. And it's going to be dangerous finding out who.*

ALL WAS quiet on the home front when Mack and I stepped through the passage into *Illusory Park*. The early morning air was moist and cool and a sense of something ominous rode the breezes wafting past.

We decided to stay in our feline forms because we could cover ground more quickly and sense changes in the air better. We hit the perimeter barrier at a dead run, the energy snapping against our skin and then falling away as we landed on the sidewalk outside of *Familiar, Inc.*

Instinct made me stop, the fur along my back lifting with alarm.

A dark haze surrounded the building, rising into the sky high above its uppermost floors.

I sensed dark, oily evil riding the haze.

My grandmama's face flashed in front of me, her expression dire. It wasn't the first time Celeste had sent me such a warning. Though her cautions generally included some kind of word puzzle that only I could solve. I didn't need to hear the words to know what she was telling me. But I did wonder if the warning meant that Grandmama was still alive.

*This is not good.* I told Mack.

*What do you want to do?*

I thought about it for a moment and then made a decision. *I'm going to confront it head on. I'll pretend I don't know what's going on and stall them for as long as I can. I'll try to get a feel for what's happening. You hang back, stay in your feline form and wait for the others. When they get here we'll decide how best to tackle this.*

*Are you sure you want to go inside alone, LA?*

*No. But something's telling me it's the right play.* I couldn't very well explain to him that I was getting flashes of my possibly dead grandmother's image. He'd think I'd lost my mind.

*I just need to do one thing first.*

Without waiting for Mack's response, I moved into the haze surrounding *Familiar, Inc.* and put myself into the shadows for protection. Then I allowed my feline form to slide away and flashed back to human.

The change was quick and mostly painless, which told me I'd been doing far too much of it of late. It was getting easier.

I wasn't sure that was a good thing.

Closing my eyes, I reached out and touched the warm, slightly electric surface of the wall before me, sending my sensing energy into it and opening my receptors fully to accept whatever readings I received.

The moment I opened myself up to it, the energy slammed into me, sending me back onto my heels. I dug in and forced myself to stay open to it, riding out the initial burst of sensation and emotions that battered my system.

Shock, fear, a feeling of betrayal, all mixed with a heightened sense of excitement tinged with dark energy. I focused harder, driving toward the dark power in the hopes of keying in on its source.

Rage burst over me, infusing my system like a million, tiny needles that caused my pulse to flare. Anger infused the air, emanating from several different sources, but focused like a laser on one entity in particular. I followed that focused emotion, riding it across a space that felt like the council chambers. I dug deeper into my sensing power, adding a touch of tracking magic to heighten the results.

My perspective shifted…rolled underneath me and left me panting on the ground. My chest burned with hate. My skin crawled with a dozen sources of magic trying to penetrate a barrier I'd created to keep it away.

I threw out a hand and watched as a bolt of unimaginable power shot from my fingertips, sailing across the well-known space and hitting its target.

I cried out, stumbling backward and slamming into the wall as the target looked up at me, eyes widening in sudden recognition, and shock, and then folded beneath the attack and fell.

*LA?*

I forced the image away, dragging myself back to the place where I stood, a young man with dark gold hair and pretty green eyes staring down at me with a worried look.

Mack touched my arm but I shrank away, mewling pitifully.

"What did you see?"

I shook my head, pressing myself against the wall as tears fled down my cheeks. "I can't…" I shot a tortured glance upward. "Celeste!"

He frowned. "What about her? Is she alive?"

I sobbed before I could stop myself, the sound reverberating through the haze as if in a cavern. "I killed her! How could I have done that?"

"You haven't killed Celeste," Mack told me. "You would never do such a thing."

"But I saw…" Then the meaning of the vision came to me, hitting me in the center of the chest like a punch. "It wasn't me." I'd somehow put myself into the killer's perspective. I shoved to my feet. "I have to go." I ran past Mack and toward the door at the side of the tall building that housed our family business. It was hidden by a tall row of evergreens and the door was always unlocked so shifters could get inside.

The room had lockers lining all four walls, with two wooden benches down the center.

The locker room was filled with clothing that could be donned after a shift. I grabbed the nearest locker, not even bothering to try to locate my own, and pulled a soft, cotton dress out of it, slipping it over my head as I ran for the door.

I took the back elevators to the Council Room level on seventeen. The elevator stopped and I pulled energy into my fingertips.

As the door slid open I looked up into the surprising face of Adriel, the demon who'd helped us in *Axismundi*. "Adriel, what are you doing here?"

"I'm helping. Trudy sent me. Come on." He motioned down the hall, toward the council chambers. "She and your mother are waiting."

I fought with myself for a moment, feeling strangely let down that the drama I'd been expecting wasn't going to happen.

But then relief filled me at the realization that what I'd seen must not have been real. I let the energy in my fingers sizzle away and fell in beside Adriel. "How did you get here?"

He glanced my way and gave me a half smile, the expression strange in his demonic face. "The council came to get Trudy and she asked me to come along to protect her."

"But the last I heard you'd gone to the border to help save your people."

He nodded, reaching for the door into the chambers. "When Reginald grabbed your friend, I followed him back to the catacombs. I was glad to have been there in time to save him."

I frowned. That meant Trudy had still been in *Axismundi* when Reggie captured us in the catacombs...

Adriel threw open the door and I stepped through.

A horrifying sight met me. But before I could make sense

of it, Adriel snapped his wrist and a long, coiled whip wrapped around my shoulders, jerking me to a halt and locking my arms to my sides. "Not so fast, LA." He grinned when I glared in his direction, nodding toward the whip. "You seem far too able to blast through the cuffs. But this whip is warded with stronger magic. You won't get free of it."

"We'll see about that," I grumbled.

Adriel glanced across the room. "Silence. I believe my king has something he'd like to say."

Growling in rage, I jerked my gaze in King Al's direction. "You bastard!"

He smiled, his handsome face a much more appropriate canvas for the gesture than Adriel's had been. "I'm sorry, my dear. Believe me when I say that I would have preferred another outcome."

"Brock's going to kill you," I growled out, though, even as I said the words I wasn't sure. Was blood thicker than loyalty and friendship?

I turned my head, my heart heavy as I looked around the room at the dozens of massive demon soldiers, every face taut with a smug sort of rage. They stood three deep around the walls and, as Adriel and I had entered the room, they'd fallen in behind us, cutting off any escape I might have considered.

But I had no intention of leaving that room.

I cast a tearful gaze over my mother and the other members of the ruling council. They'd been cuffed with the magic dampening bracelets. The ones who'd tried to fight back were lying on the floor, deathly still.

Tears fell from my eyes as I saw that my mother was among them. She was so pale. Like Celeste had been the last time I'd seen her.

The thought brought my head up, the pieces of the puzzle snapping together. "You killed Celeste. She was getting better and you hit her with enough energy to drain her remaining strength."

King Al looked down at the table. His wide mouth twisted unhappily. "She was a good friend. I hated to do it, you must believe that, LA."

I shook my head, tears rolling down my cheeks. "Why didn't she tell mother or me what you'd done?"

"She would have, surely," he said. "But I informed her that I would kill you both. Her silence was the price paid for your lives."

"And yet you still killed my mother!" I could barely see for the tears flooding from my eyes.

"She lives, LA."

Despite myself I closed my eyes, sighing in relief. Then I snapped them open. "I'm surprised you didn't just slaughter her and be done with it. She's not going to just walk away and let you take over the council."

"I'd much rather have her at my side, my dear. But that will be up to her."

I bit back the words I wanted to scream. That my mother would never bow to him or any other. That she came from a long line of powerful Familiars and she'd fight him to the death. I couldn't say those words because I was afraid.

Afraid he'd just kill her and be done with it.

Afraid I was wrong.

I wasn't sure I'd be able to live with it if she *did* give in.

So, I changed the subject. "How did you get the key to the other dimension?"

His expression was smug, though I could tell he tried to fight it. He was proud of his trickery. "I'm surprised you haven't figured that out by now."

But I had. "Star. She pulled it from the web when she ravaged it."

He nodded. "Very good. It was buried in the protections, infused into the warding."

I shook my head, suddenly feeling so tired. "I hope you're consumed by the power you've grabbed. I hope it tears you to pieces. Your treachery won't be forgotten. I can promise you that." My eyes scanned past my mother and I saw the slight, stooped figure standing at the back of the room. Bracketed by guards who held her upright between them, Trudy's head was down, her hands folded in front of her. She appeared to be staring at the ground.

"Are you part of this, aunt?"

For a long moment she didn't respond. Then I saw her shudder, her narrow shoulders rounding just a bit more before she lifted her head.

I gasped at her face, which was framed in blood that ran from wounds beneath her hair. She stared at me through eyes that were dark with rage. Her beautiful mouth was tight with it, and I finally recognized the shimmer in her frame as being rage rather than the weakness I'd thought it was.

I longed to reach for her mind with my energy but I couldn't. Not with my arms trapped.

Something shifted over Trudy's gaze and I started. I'd seen it before.

The shadow passed over her again. I recognized the dark, restless energy squatting within her frame and I nearly smiled.

Holding my aunt's fierce gaze, I nodded slightly.

"Why do you look so pleased with yourself, my dear," King Al asked. When I glanced his way, I saw the worry written in his expression and knew. Despite his brave words, and the outward appearance that he'd won, he wasn't entirely comfortable. I had to wonder why. "Where is Celeste?"

He feigned sadness. "I thought you knew, child. She

passed. I believe she's resting comfortably in the *Elysian Fields* about now."

I seriously doubted that.

"If she *is*, your betrayal will wrench her back to this world."

He shook his head, giving me a pitying look. "You know that's not possible, LA."

"Isn't it?" I took great pleasure in the doubt that formed lines between his heavy black brows.

The king jerked his head toward Adriel. "Take her. We'll let her calm down for a while." The king stood from his chair and gave me a benevolent smile. "I'll see you at dinner, my dear."

Static filled my head and agony sizzled up my arms. I gritted my teeth against the pain, knowing what it meant. "I'm staying here. You and I need to talk."

He blinked, clearly surprised by my attitude. I was surprised too. I really should have been a drooling puddle on the floor by that point. But if Trudy was going to pull off what she needed to pull off, she'd need my help.

I sent Deg a quick thought, biting back a cry as I delivered the SOS. Flames burst from the whip and sizzled against my arm. I screamed and fell to my knees, using the opportunity to position myself closer to Adriel.

"You should know better," he whispered as he leaned down.

I made myself heavy, my hand grasping the tail of his armored coat. As he jerked me upright, I grasped the hilt of his sword and pulled it free of its sheath.

With one, quick flick of my wrist I sliced it across Adriel's wrist. He released the whip and it fell away.

I spun, screaming. "Now!"

Trudy's form straightened with a jerk as I swung the blade at the next guard. They were moving in on me in a wad, their hands filled with swords and their gazes bulging with hate.

I kept them at a distance until I saw the wraith slide from Trudy's slender form and swoop toward the King. The shadow dove toward him, sliding easily into his big body.

He jerked upright with an enraged bellow, effectively drawing the guards' attention to himself.

I wounded a few more while they were looking away and then took a deep breath and screamed. "Down!"

Pulling copiously from Deg and my shared power, I yanked my energy forward and let it explode outward on a power word. "*Confusio!*"

Guards blew away from me like leaves on a brisk wind.

I rose into the air under the destructive power, spinning helplessly as it burned itself out. Furniture flew away from my power vacuum, slamming into the massive guards and knocking them against each other.

It was a desperate move, meant only to create chaos and discombobulate the guards. I had nothing left to follow it up with once everything settled down and the guards pulled themselves back together.

I prayed my friends would hurry. They were near. I could feel them.

Beyond the commotion, the king was screaming as Celeste had her spiritual way with him, no doubt terrifying him with her heavy hand on his brain.

The door blew open and I slammed to the ground, my energy washed away in a wave of fresh magic.

My friends flooded into the room, along with some I would have never expected, including Trudy's handsome soldier.

I made a mental note to get the story on him. But in that moment, I had something more important to do. I crawled toward the injured council members, mother first, and pulled them under the heavy council table for protection. I was pleased to discover that only a couple of them were beyond help. I hoped with the Nephilim's healing powers and some time, they'd recover completely.

I wrapped myself around my mother and rested, my back against the leg of the table. I watched my friends kick the demons' butts and wished I had the energy to help. But my explosion of power had taken it out of me.

It was all I could do to just sit there and admire the view.

To my relief, Brock was one of the most aggressive of the council's defenders. That made me happy.

Mandy and Deg did me proud with their seamless magical attacks. And, when I spared King Al a glance, I saw that Celeste had him well in hand.

He was slumped in a corner of the room, babbling to himself and twitching at shadows.

I couldn't help grinning. It never paid to underestimate a Mapes.

# CHAPTER TWENTY

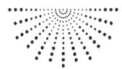

*S*itting on the large flat rock in the center of my sanctuary, I watched a new group of kittens play with a fuzzy ball I'd thrown out for them.

Observing their silly antics made me feel a bit better, though I'd been deep in depression for the last week, since I'd had to face the fact that Celeste was truly gone.

Yes, she'd pulled some strings at the *Elysian Fields* to come back as a wraith. But that had been extenuating circumstances, no doubt aided and abetted by Mabel, who had some pull in the right places. But I figured that would be the last I saw of Celeste. At least for a while.

And that made me sad.

Though I'd spent a large part of my adult life trying to avoid the strings attached to my family, I'd come to know… too late of course…just how much they contributed to my sense of self and happiness.

I sighed as the smallest kitten snagged the ball out from under the pink nose of the largest one and finally grinned as she flattened her bigger sibling when he tried to get it back. The four fuzzy babies scampered away, to the spot in the sun where their less social mother lie resting from her recent ordeal on the streets.

I'd made some progress with the distrustful feline over the last several days, but her animus toward the human type critters in her universe was deep seated. It would take us some time to become friends.

A feat I fully intended to pull off.

The interior door into the sanctuary opened and closed quietly behind me. I knew who it was before she joined me on the sun-warmed rock.

Mother reached for my hand and clasped it as she eased into a spot next to me. "How are you, Peaches?"

I bit back my usual, too fast, response of "I'm fine," and answered truthfully instead. "I miss her."

Mother sighed. "Me too. But I know she's very proud of you. What you did for us..." Queen Katherine sighed. "Well, it took more courage than I think I'd have had under the circumstances."

I frowned. "I didn't do anything."

She gave me her patented look. "LA, I tested my powers against Reginald's cuffs. I know how much it hurt to go against them." She frowned. "Trudy told me those cuffs are impossible to beat. Yet, according to your friends, you did it several times. How did you manage it?"

I shrugged. "Darned if I know. It happened by accident the first time and I just kind of figured, I had nothing to lose by trying it again."

Mother's red-gold brows arched. "The first time?" She patted my hand. "You amaze me."

We sat quietly watching the kittens play for a few minutes. Mother laughed heartily at the antics of the tiny female. "I like her. If you're looking for a home for her, I'd love to have a cat again. I've missed the company."

"Mama Cat and I haven't discussed it yet but I'll put in a good word for you."

Mother grinned. "Thanks, Peaches."

"How's Trudy?" I asked. I'd kept my distance from my aunt since the day in the council chambers. I wasn't sure how I felt about her yet. Even if she'd had nothing to do with King Al's treachery, she'd surely been a part of the plot on some level. And I might have lost my mother because of her duplicity.

"Physically she's healthy. But emotionally…" mother shrugged. "I think she was hoping to see Celeste again."

"She kind of saw her up close and personal," I said, grinning.

Mother shuddered. "Don't remind me. Ew."

I laughed softly. Resting my head on her shoulder, I gave myself up to the pleasure of just being with her. But in the back of my mind was the usual question when my mother showed up unannounced. *Why is she really here?*

She finally fessed up so I wouldn't have to ask. "Which brings me to the reason I've come…"

I lifted my head and gave her my full attention.

She stared at the kittens for a beat and then turned to me. Her pretty blue-green gaze, so like Celeste's, was filled with uncertainty.

It was a look I wasn't used to seeing in my mother's eyes.

"I wanted you to be the first to know. I'm stepping down as the figurehead on the council."

I stared at her, trying to determine from her expression exactly what she was telling me. "You aren't going to be queen anymore?"

She shrugged. "You and I both know that was just a title. There are no real kings and queens in our world. It was just a way to indicate a hierarchy. But I'm not so sure that's a good idea anymore."

Realization hit me. "This is Trudy's work."

"I won't deny she's had some influence on me. But I was really considering this change before she arrived back home. With mother's passing…"

Grief crept over her pretty face. She took a deep breath and straightened her shoulders. "I supported the practice for her. Because she'd earned the position. She was the strongest woman I've ever known. I couldn't possibly fill her shoes…"

"That's not true," I objected.

She held up a hand. "Nor would I want to. I want something entirely different. And that's why I've come to see you, LA. It became crystal clear to me during this latest crisis just how much we depend on our young ones. You, the Witches and Brock saved us. You put yourselves in great danger to protect us from ourselves. You should not be relegated to the sidelines any longer. More importantly, I want fresh blood on the council."

She touched my arm as I felt my pulse speed. There was no way she was suggesting what I thought she was suggesting.

I started to shake my head.

"Don't say no. Not without giving it some thought. And just to be clear, I'm not suggesting that only you join the council. I want your friends too."

I was speechless with shock.

Mother stood up and nodded. "I know it's a lot to take in so I'll leave you to think about it."

The outer door opened and Deg came through. He ground to a halt when he spotted mother. "Queen Katherine."

She shook her head, giving me a look filled with sadness, and then left.

Deg waited until the door closed behind her to ask. "Is she all right?"

"I think she will be. She just has a lot on her mind. And with Celeste…" I shook my head.

Deg sat down next to me and the kittens immediately ran over to attack his shoe laces. He scooped a tiger striped male up and nuzzled it against his face. After a moment he looked into my eyes. "How about you? Are you okay? I'm worried about you."

I bumped him with my shoulder. "I will be too. I just miss her a lot, you know."

"I do know. If you need to talk…"

I nodded.

A pretty white female with startling blue eyes leapt at the tiger and the two of them had a spirited game of bat-face before the female got bored and scampered away. The little tiger curled up in Deg's lap and promptly fell asleep. "Are you going to tell me what's going on with the queen?" he asked with studied nonchalance.

I frowned. It was strange thinking about mother's title going away. But I did like the idea of the new order. It made sense. And while it would make some in *Illusion City* unhappy, it would probably please a lot more. "I'll let her tell you. She has big news."

His expression was filled with curiosity, but he didn't press. "I understand Trudy's staying."

"Yes. Mother thinks she can help."

"But you don't agree?"

"Let's just say I'm going to be keeping an eye on my Auntie."

"Probably wise. We still don't really know if she was working with Reginald."

I realized I hadn't gotten the scoop on that. "So, what happened after I left? I haven't seen Mabel or her brothers. Are they safe?"

"For now. When the Heavenly realm discovered how

close they'd been to being breached because of the Nephilim, the three youngsters were recalled."

"Did Al really use Ralph and Mack to breach the other dimensions?"

"Reggie couldn't get them to cooperate. But they were imprisoned in the catacombs with us and they used them for leverage."

I frowned. "Then how did they breach the other dimensions?"

"They didn't. It was a big magic show to make the council believe all was lost. Al was working them hard, trying to talk them into giving up without a fight. He was willing to take us by force, but if he could pull it off without a fight so much the better."

"Jerk." Then I realized what he was telling me. "He only wanted the human dimension."

"Well, to be accurate, Reginald wanted the Heavenly realm too. But this is where the real power and opportunity is. Humans are an untapped resource and the mix of supernaturals here makes for a vibrant society. We're the key to the future and the other dimensions all know it."

Deg's finger moved rhythmically, scratching the kitten under its chin as it purred and stretched.

"I'm sorry about Mabel. I kind of liked having her around."

"Me too. I have a feeling, knowing Miss Mabel, that she'll be back."

We shared a grin.

"What happened to ol' Reggie?" I asked, my grin widening.

"He's currently residing in his catacombs with King Al." Deg said happily. "We thought it was a fitting punishment for the two of them."

"Absolutely. I guess he was hoping to get control of *Axismundi*?"

"Maybe. But I think he'd set his sights a bit higher. Al promised him the Heavenly realm if he helped. Between you and me, I have my doubts about whether he would have honored that promise."

"Ha! So much for equality," I scoffed. "I think you're probably right about Al stabbing him in the back. Those two are a couple of snakes."

"They are for sure," Deg agreed.

"I wonder who'll take Trudy's spot in the afterlife?"

"For now, Ebbot, her boyfriend will keep things running in *Mundala*."

"The hand...erm...the guard she seemed so chummy with?"

Deg lifted a dark brow and then nodded. "Yes. He never turned against her, I guess. He was working with Reggie as a spy. He was the one who warned Mabel about Reggie's plans to lock us in the catacombs."

"And Mabel went along with capturing me because Reggie had her brothers?"

" Yes. But Ebbot told her where she could find them and she released them with us. They apparently assumed Reggie would be easier to sneak up on if he thought he was running unopposed."

"Seems they were right. He was freakishly cocky."

"Yes. He was."

"Adriel?"

Deg shook his head. "That one confused me. I have no idea why he helped us initially and then turned on us."

"Maybe he was straddling both sides in case King Al's plans failed."

"Or until he figured out which side would benefit him

most?" Deg nodded. "It's possible. From everything I've heard, Adriel's loyalties are transferable. He's a bit of a wild card. Brock told me the demons in the demonic realm didn't believe ol' Al could pull it off. If Adriel had doubts that would make sense."

"How is he? Brock?"

Deg sighed. "You can imagine how disappointed he is in his uncle. But I think it bothers him more that people are now looking at him like he's part of the resistance."

I realized my mother would have probably known that and I wondered if it had factored into her decision to add us to the council. "I think that might change soon."

"You know something?"

"Yeah. But it's not my news to tell."

Deg settled the sleeping kitten back onto the grass and stood. "I need to go. Talk to you later?"

"Absolutely."

He stopped at the door, turning back. "There is one other thing, LA."

I swung around to look at him.

"Brock and Mandy don't want to tell you, but I thought you should know."

"Now you're worrying me. What is it?"

"You know how they won't tell us how they got back here when we thought they were dead?"

I nodded.

"They won't because they can't. Mandy admitted to me that she fell into that bog and was sinking, something dark and deadly wrapping itself around her, and then something happened and she suddenly found herself lying near the border of *Illusory Park*."

"How's that possible?"

He shrugged. "No idea. She said there was a flash of light and then she was out of the bog. Brock told me a similar story. He was being attacked by those things in the sky and suddenly there was a flash of light and he was lying in the primordial forest."

"What about the wraith?"

"Huh?"

"Remember they told us they thought they'd seen a wraith when they came back?"

"Oh. Yeah. They described it to me as a shadow sliding away from them after they came to in the park." He shrugged. "Anyway, I thought you should know. I guess that's a mystery for another day."

I nodded and watched him leave, my mind spinning.

The sanctuary was eerily quiet after he left. I sat a moment longer, trying to make sense of something that clearly didn't. I finally gave up, figuring I'd tackle it when I wasn't so tired.

I sat a while longer, lacking the energy to do my chores, and then forced myself to stand. I was heading for the house when I heard a soft sound behind me.

I turned in time to see a shadow skimming along the glass ceiling.

My pulse surged for a beat and then I caught a glimpse of the pale, wispy form standing a few feet away.

I gave a small yelp of surprise.

Celeste grinned, pushing at her ethereal wave of red-gold hair with one hand. "That bad, huh?"

I grinned. "Grandmama!" I took a couple of steps in her direction but her image wavered so I stopped, afraid I'd cause her to disappear entirely.

"How are you, child?"

"Better now. How's life in the *Elysian Fields*?"

"Boring," she complained happily. "But there are perks." She cast a meaningful glance toward the wraith perched in the branches of the sanctuary's biggest tree. "I have my very own taxi service."

I laughed. Leave it to Celeste to arrange things to her liking, even after death. "I don't think that's how they're supposed to be used."

She shrugged. "A strong will is a strong will, child. Even in the afterlife."

I nodded, suddenly feeling the shame I'd nursed since leaving her on her deathbed to rush back to Trudy. "I...I'm really sorry I abandoned you."

Celeste's gaze held the maturity of centuries of life. She smiled gently. "Don't apologize. You were tending to the affairs of the living. I no longer belong in that world."

Tears burned my eyes.

She shook her head. "Don't cry for me, child. I'm happy. I have a whole new group of people to terrorize here. It's delightful."

I gave a watery laugh. "I don't believe you."

She lifted perfect, red-gold brows. I was happy to see that she'd regained her beauty and vitality after her death. It seemed right. "Have you met me?"

"I mean about the being happy part. The terrorizing part is a given."

She chuckled darkly. "But I *am* happy. I would never lie to you, LA. I *have* never lied to you. You do know that, right?"

I sniffled, scraping tears off my cheeks. "I miss you so much."

"I miss you too, child. And your mother." She frowned and I wondered if she was thinking of Trudy. "We'll still see each other. I promise."

"I'm glad."

Her image shivered on the air and I held my breath, but it strengthened again and I blinked, realizing she was only a couple of feet away. Grandmama reached out and touched my hands, grasping them in a cool, firm grip. I looked into her pretty face and felt my world evening out again. "I came because I wanted to tell you two very important things."

I nodded. "I'm listening."

"Number one." Her gaze softened. "I'm oh so proud of you, child. You are every bit the woman and Familiar that I'd hoped you'd become."

I didn't even try to stop the tears as they ran from my eyes. Sniffling, I allowed myself to be pulled into her arms. Despite the coolness of her frame, the hug warmed me to the center of my heart. "Thank you, Grandmama."

"And number two," she said, pulling out of the hug and fixing me with a stern look. "Things are changing. Challenges continue to build in your world. Do not let your guard down and know whom you can trust at all times. It's vital that you heed my words, child."

A million questions popped into my head.

But I wasn't going to be allowed to ask them.

Almost as soon as the last word drifted from between her lips, Celeste started to fade away.

"Goodbye, LA. I'll see you soon."

I bit back a sob, covering my mouth with my fingers to keep from begging her to stay. I knew she'd moved on to the next phase of her long, long existence.

I needed to do the same.

But as the wraith swooped through the sanctuary, bathing me in cool air that made me shiver violently, I knew I would always have Celeste in my corner, no matter what happened.

That was a balm to my sorrow. "I love you Grandmama," I whispered to the empty air.

Her voice danced back to me through the stillness, filled with the warmth her form no longer held. *I love you too, child.*

# READ MORE RELUCTANT FAMILIAR MYSTERIES

If you enjoyed **A Familiar Problem**, you'll love the next book in this fun series. **Familiar Hijinks**.

*This year, for Christmas, LA's definitely feeling more jammed up than joyful.*

When someone infects human Santa Claus stand-ins with magic they can't control, Christmas suddenly becomes more menacing than merry. The last thing LA needs is to deal with a disaster that might bring the whole human population to their doorstep with pitchforks and torches.

She's woefully behind on her gift shopping. Her Aunt Trudy is keeping secrets. And a certain, bossy police detective is definitely *not* what he seems.

LA and Deg must work their way through a suspect list that includes some pretty heavy hitters in the magical and mythological realms, and find the proverbial strand of tinsel on the tree that leads to the troublemaker.

It's starting to look a lot like crisis, and a pair of rosy cheeks and a jolly giggle might not be enough to keep the Peace on Earth this year.

# FAMILIAR HIJINKS

## CHAPTER ONE

*Wake up, LeeAnn!*

My grandmama's face appeared in front of mine; her blue-green eyes narrowed with irritation. She reached up and tapped me hard on the nose. *Wake up! You've got things to do.*

I snorted awake, opening my eyes to find myself surrounded by white; a pristine glow emanating from beyond the window in my bedroom.

I sniffled, shoving a fire-colored rats-nest out of my face and sitting up. I'd asked my grandmama to make sure I woke up early because, she was right, it was Christmas Eve and I was woefully behind on my shopping. Using one's dead grandmama as an alarm clock was admittedly strange, but Celeste was bored in the Elysian Fields and she didn't mind.

"Thanks, Celeste!" I muttered around a yawn.

A soft voice danced through the impossible brightness of my room. *You're welcome, child.*

Sighing expansively, I shoved the covers back. I sat on the

edge of my bed and looked out at the unrelieved white beyond my window.

"Ugh."

Snowing again. It seemed as though it had done nothing but drop snow and ice on our heads for weeks. The ground outside the shabby, careworn brownstone I called home was thick with the stuff. It covered all but a narrow ribbon of the sidewalks and roads, people and cars fighting for that limited space as we tried to go about our business, preparing for the holidays.

Which reminded me. I shoved to my feet, groaning as the last several days of training with Deg, a.k.a. Deggart Kincaide, my Witch, came back to bite me on the butt. Literally. My cheeks were killing me.

I yawned, heading to the bathroom to pee and brush the cotton from my teeth.

I spotted the clock on my dresser as I passed, groaning. I was late. I'd promised my friends I'd meet them at our favorite downtown diner for breakfast before we did our Christmas shopping. I needed to be there in fifteen minutes.

That's what I got for using a ghost as an alarm clock. They had horrible time perception on the Earthly plane.

My friends and I had decided to do our shopping together so we'd be sure to get something each of us wanted. We'd exchanged names in our own version of Secret Santa… only it wasn't so secret.

I did my thing in the bathroom, adding a quick, hot shower to the "to do" list while there. Hopefully, the hot water would ease some of the achiness from my overused muscles. Then I headed to the kitchen for coffee.

Firing up the small TV on my kitchen counter, I watched the news while my coffee brewed. I stared blankly at the usual reports of endless snow, grimacing and complaining aloud to a weather lady, who was dressed as if she lived on the beach. I was sipping the first cup of hot sweet and creamy coffee, thinking about heading into my cat sanctuary to feed my current residents...of which there were legions thanks to the never-ending snow...when the first news report of spilled magic hit the airwaves and filtered through my half-asleep brain cells.

The images flashed from ambulances and police cars to a pair of EMTs crouched in the snow, bent over someone on a stretcher.

The emergency medical responders tugged the stretcher upward, engaging its wheels so they could roll it to the waiting ambulance. A meaty hand, the fingers black with some kind of soot, fell off one side of the stretcher as it bounced over snow and ice.

I started to leave the kitchen but stopped in the door as a deep voice came on and spoke the words everyone in the magic world has dreaded since merging our fates with those in the human realm.

"I don't know what happened. It was like lightning flew out of his fingertips," the voice said. "He must have been holding one of those laser things in his hand. It's the only explanation."

I turned to the worried-sounding man on the television screen. He had dark skin and thick black brows that were lowered over chocolate brown eyes. "The lightning seared a woman's bag right off at the handles and burned a streak in her arm." He shook his head. "I've never seen anything like that."

I forgot the mug in my hand and the chores on my list. Patting my jeans for my phone, I realized I hadn't grabbed it from my bedside table.

As I was rushing back to get the phone, it started ringing.

I didn't bother with pleasantries when I recognized Deg's name on the screen. "You saw?"

"Yes. I'll pick you up in five minutes."

If I hurried, I'd just have time to throw some food into the cats' bowls before he got there.

The offices of *Familiar, Inc.* were unusually busy when Deg and I hit the lobby. Magical creatures of every kind moved from office to office with urgent steps, wearing identical looks of concern on their faces.

A small group of people I didn't know clustered near the elevator, their voices buzzing over some kind of news.

I figured I knew what the news was. I wasn't wrong.

"That makes the tenth event this month," a dark-haired woman whose petite stature and slightly pointed ears put her firmly in the elf column. I had to sense her aura though to determine whether she was of the light variety or the dark.

Despite human fables and lore, dark fairies and elves weren't inherently more evil than light. Though those whose bloodlines originated on the darker side of the spectrum seemed slightly more inclined to make bad choices.

The term, "bad choices" being magic-speak for actions that harmed the human population we were sworn to protect.

A tall man with spiky black hair shook his head at her words. "Eleven now. We've had two incidents this morning."

Deg and I shared a look.

"Excuse me," I interrupted. "There was a second one?"

Several heads nodded. The elf spoke up. "The one on the street downtown, and there was another one at the mall, in the toy store there." Her expression was so dark I had a moment's panic.

"Children?"

She shook her head. "No kids were hurt. But one of the clerks is fighting for her life at the hospital right now."

"Dangit," I murmured. What in the worlds was going on?

Deg punched the number for the seventeenth floor...the council chambers. We didn't speak until we'd entered the car and the doors had slid closed. Then I looked at him. "This is bad."

He nodded. "I'm wondering if we aren't looking at something from Underworld again."

I didn't even want to think about that. But there was still the open issue of the wraiths—or something magical that appeared like wraiths—which had recently followed our friends Brock and Mandy back from Underworld.

"I'm leaning toward it being a troublemaker closer to home. Like an ex-council-member," I told him.

My mother, the former Queen of the magic users in the human realm, had recently flattened out the council because of some dirty dealings by at least one of its members. She'd brought in new blood, in the form of me and my three friends, Deg, Mandy and Brock, to represent the younger, more open-minded segment of our magical population on Earth. As a sad...or happy depending on your outlook... result of that change, some of the older magic houses had been excused from council service.

It seemed highly likely one of them could be behind the current issues.

The elevator stopped on the seventeenth floor.

Deg nodded as the doors slid open. "That probably makes more sense." He looked around and lowered his voice before adding, "Or someone who's still on the council but doesn't like the direction your mother's taking it."

I knew he was thinking of his own leader, Serena. The High Priestess of the coven for the human realm had been very vocal in her opposition to the new order. And she'd already been unhappy because of my family's role on the council. She believed Familiars belonged on a rung somewhere below the Witches. And she'd been guilty of questionable, if not borderline illegal, tactics in the past to undermine our work.

"Whoever it is," I murmured back, "we need to figure it out really fast and put a stop to it. The human police aren't stupid. They're going to realize pretty quickly that things aren't adding up."

Deg opened the door for me, and we slipped through as the stairwell entrance down the hall opened and slammed shut. I glanced that way, finding a recognizable form striding toward us.

Brock did *not* look happy.

I looked into his dark gaze and lifted my brows as he strode in our direction. He gave his head a quick shake and moved past us. The demon didn't go directly to his seat behind the council table. Instead, he headed for my mother.

Katherine Mapes was standing at the back of the room, talking to a woman who looked a lot like her and…I've been told…like me too.

Aunt Trudy was looking remarkably better than she had when she'd returned from Underworld a few weeks earlier. Her gray-blue gaze locked on us and her narrow shoulders straightened as Brock hurried in their direction. As he stopped before them, Trudy's eyes found me and, as they had nearly every time since her return to the human realm, filled with speculation.

I wondered at her continued coldness, figuring it was most likely based in uncertainty about my opinion of her return.

A not unreasonable uncertainty, since I didn't know myself how I felt about it.

Deg and I joined the small group at the back of the room.

As we did, I could feel the curious and hostile glances from the other council members searing the back of my head.

"What's going on?" I asked my mother.

She nodded toward Brock.

He frowned. "The human police are here. They're downstairs in the lobby."

Panic clawed my gut at the news. "Already? How'd they track the magic leakage back here so quickly?"

His gaze grew dark. "It's worse than that. They shouldn't have been able to trace it to us at all." He skimmed a quick look to Trudy. "As you requested, I visited the hospital where the victims were taken. I was prepared to intervene before the doctors could examine the magic users…"

I held up a hand. "How were you going to do that without drawing even more attention to us?"

"I gave him a spell," Mandy said in her snotty tone of voice.

Of course, she had.

"Befuddlement?" Deg asked in typical witch-speak.

She nodded. "I added a thread of diarrhea to the spell." She grinned. "It's potent."

Deg chuckled, "Dang. That's just mean."

Mother fixed them with a look that tore the grins right off their faces. But then she said, "Desperate times call for desperate measures."

We all laughed.

Everyone except for Brock. "As I was saying…" He slid a quelling look over us. "I didn't use the spell. The magic users were human."

There was a beat of stunned silence.

Finally, Trudy said. "That's not possible."

Brock shrugged. "I examined them myself." His frown deepened. "It's bad. Some of them are so weak from expending the foreign energy they look like living wraiths."

The seriousness of the situation hit me like a barrel filled with rocks. I'd been focusing on the danger to the magic population because of the very public aspect of the attacks. I'd neglected to give a thought to how the human vessels might be faring.

Of course, in my defense, I'd assumed they were sick or renegade magic users. Not humans. The human body is much too frail a vessel for magic.

"How?"

He shook his head. "No idea. Their auras are strictly human. There's no question. But there was something…"

"Are you going to share with the rest of the council?" A high-pitched, nasally voice said from behind me. I turned to find Serena standing there. She fixed me with a sour look; her narrow, cadaverous face made even more haggard by the disgusted puckering of her thin lips. "I thought we were done with secrets on the council."

Mother nodded. "You're right, Serena. I'm afraid we got caught up in the moment. Brock has some distressing news for us." She nodded toward her sister.

Aunt Trudy gave Serena a long look, her lips compressed into a thin line as the High Priestess met her stare head-on.

"Trudy," Mother said.

My aunt finally shifted her gaze to her sister. "Of course." She moved to sit down at the table. Her spot was next to Serena's, a fact that probably had a lot to do with their ongoing animus, and at Mother's right hand. Though Katherine Mapes had given up her virtual crown in an effort to create a more evenly weighted council, she'd kept her seat at the center of the table.

I figured it was because too much change at one time would have created its own kind of chaos in the room.

When we were all seated, Mother turned to Trudy. "Would you give your report, please?"

Trudy nodded, standing. Her gaze slid around the room and landed on me. Brock, Deg, Mandy and I sat together on one end, an island of common sense in a sea of egos. Mother had been against our sitting together at first, but she relented when she realized how much pushback we were going to be getting from the elders.

We needed to show a united front, or they'd eat us alive.

"I wanted to assure the council that what is going on right now has nothing to do with Underworld. I contacted all of my sources there and the response was unanimous. There are currently no plots to undermine or overwhelm our position here." As was her way since being offered a seat at the council table, Trudy gave her information in short, unadulterated bursts and then kept her silence. Though her gaze was watchful and speculative at all times.

I knew she kept most of her council private. I'd seen her and my mother with their heads together after every council meeting. And by the way Serena watched the two women at the center of the table, I knew she'd noticed it too.

The arrangement wasn't exactly conducive to healthy council relations. However, I was willing to give Trudy some time to adjust. She'd never been good at sharing her toys.

"Brock, would you fill the council in on what you learned, please?"

Brock stood and repeated what he'd told us.

Gasps of horror and surprise rose around the table when he revealed that the magic users had been human.

"This is an outrage!" Serena exclaimed in her strident, sinus-heavy tones. "We have to get to the bottom of it immediately."

I thought my mother showed great restraint. "Yes, we do, Serena. That's why we're here."

Serena's response was a tightening of her thin, cruel lips as anger flashed in her nearly black gaze.

"You say the human police are downstairs?" the Elven King asked. We all turned toward King Markland, noting the multi-hued sparks dancing on the air around his head. When elves got upset, they tended to shed magic dust.

Fortunately, the human population seemed oblivious to it.

But for us, it was a bit of a nuisance. Magic dust was highly allergenic.

As if reading my thoughts, the man sitting next to Markland sneezed, his chin nearly hitting the table under the violence of it. "Sorry," he murmured, running a pristine square of white linen under his bulbous nose.

I grinned at the King of the Trolls. His wide, craggy face turned pink as he returned my smile.

"They're speaking to our first level resistance now. But the Detective in charge concerns me a little. He's very..." Brock frowned as if searching for the right word. "Determined, is the nicest word I can come up with."

"First level contains our best people," King Eglund of the Troll People mused. His nose twitched and he fell into another long series of sneezes that left him groaning. "So sorry."

Mother gave King Markland a look. "Contain your dust, Markland."

The Elven king pasted a regal look on his handsome face and reached up to pinch a pointy ear. The cloud of dust disappeared. "Best people or not, I'm concerned they managed to track the problem back to us. It's the first step on the short road to discovery."

Heads up and down the table nodded.

Deg sat forward. "If you'd like, Mandy and I can put ourselves in the vicinity and see what we can discover."

Mother looked at Serena, since, as head of the witches, technically the decision should be hers to make. She looked down her long, pointy nose and nodded. "Use your spells to remain out of sight. Report to me when you've completed your mission."

"Report to the council," Mother corrected with a quelling gaze toward the High Priestess.

Serena reluctantly dipped her head. "Of course."

I watched my friends leave the room, filled with jealousy. I wanted to be on the front lines of the investigation. Not sitting on my butt talking about…whatever we were getting ready to talk about.

"Now, we have some current business to discuss." Mother narrowed her gaze on King Eglund. "We need to discuss the bathrooms on the Troll level."

He flushed and cleared his throat. "I know they've clogged the toilets again…" he began.

Beside me, Brock groaned softly.

And with a whimper and a sigh, my soul died just a little.

## ALSO BY SAM CHEEVER

If you enjoyed **A Familiar Problem**, you might also enjoy these other fun mystery series by Sam. To find out more, visit the **BOOKS** page at www.samcheever.com:

Gainfully Employed Mysteries

Honeybun Heat Series

Silver Hills Cozy Mysteries

Country Cousin Mysteries

Yesterday's Paranormal Mysteries

Reluctant Familiar Paranormal Mysteries

# ABOUT THE AUTHOR

*USA Today and Wall Street Journal Bestselling Author* Sam Cheever writes mystery and suspense, creating stories that draw you in and keep you eagerly turning pages. Known for writing great characters, snappy dialogue, and unique and exhilarating stories, Sam is the award-winning author of 80+ books.

*To learn more about Sam and her work, visit her at one of her online hotspots:*
www.samcheever.com
samcheever@samcheever.com